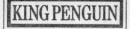

MISS PEABODY'S INHERITANCE

Born in the industrial Midlands of England in 1923, Elizabeth Jolley was brought up in a German-speaking household – her father having met her mother, the daughter of an Austrian general, when engaged on famine relief in Vienna in 1919. She was educated at home and later at a Quaker boarding-school.

In 1959 she moved to Western Australia with her husband and three children. She cultivates a small orchard and goose farm and conducts writing workshops in prisons and community centres. Having tried her hand at being a nurse, a door-to-door salesperson and a flying domestic she is now a part-time tutor in the department of English at the Western Australian Institute of Technology.

Elizabeth Jolley is the author of three short-story collections and three other novels, including *Mr Scobie's Riddle* (Penguin, 1985). Her work has been acclaimed in America as well as Australia and the UK, and the *Washington Post* called her style 'Effortlessly comic' and her characters 'Battily original'.

ELIZABETH JOLLEY

MISS PEABODY'S INHERITANCE

A KING PENGUIN
PUBLISHED BY PENGUIN BOOKS

Penguin Books Ltd, Harmondsworth, Middlesex, England
Viking Penguin Inc., 40 West 23rd Street, New York, New York 10010, U.S.A.
Penguin Books Australia Ltd, Ringwood, Victoria, Australia
Penguin Books Canada Limited, 2801 John Street, Markham, Ontario, Canada L3R 1B4
Penguin Books (N.Z.) Ltd, 182–190 Wairau Road, Auckland 10, New Zealand

First published by Viking 1984
Published in Penguin Books 1986

Made and printed in Great Britain by
Richard Clay (The Chaucer Press) Ltd,
Bungay, Suffolk
Typeset in Palatino

The final draft of this novel was completed during my time of being Writer in Residence at the Western Australian Institute of Technology.

This book is offered as an expression of thanks to the Artist in Residence Committee and, in particular, to Derek Holroyde, Brian Dibble, and Don Grant.

Miss Peabody's
Inheritance

The nights belonged to the novelist.

I have a Headmistress in mind, you know, a tremendously responsible sort of woman, the novelist's large handwriting was black on large sheets of paper. The name of the Headmistress is Dr Arabella Thorne; she is known as Miss Thorne. Every afternoon she walks down from the School House through the warm fragrance of a small pine plantation.

She always forgets about the pines and then suddenly she is in the middle of the sandy pine-needly place, walking on a little beaten path. She feels refreshed by the dry lightness of the air and the clean comforting scent from the sun-warmed trees.

It is surprising that she forgets because the school is called Pine Heights.

When Miss Thorne walks alone all kinds of things go through her head. Sometimes it is a line of poetry or a phrase from a piano concerto. Sometimes it is something wise to do with her policy in her school. She wants her students to study for pleasure and she wants them to cultivate an incredible hunger for books. She remembers something Samuel Johnson said in 1728:

> *The flesh of animals who feed excursively is allowed to have a higher flavour than that of those who are cooped up. May there not be the same difference between men who read as their taste prompts, and men who are confined in cells and colleges to stated tasks . . .*

Perhaps it was Boswell who actually said this, Miss Thorne is not sure but she resolves to speak to Miss Edgely about it and ask her to type a memo for the notice board. She will have to check the memo as Edgely is inclined now to make silly little mistakes. Not so long ago she put a *c* where a *p* should have been and left out an *l* and an *e*: " . . . *the copulation in the pubic schools is increasing at an alarming rat*". The article, to be supplied by Miss Thorne to a journal for higher education, was entirely ruined.

Sometimes, when she walks, she thinks about the girls: the new one called Debbie in her clinging jersey dress, her hair

1

cut long over her eyes and the way she has of throwing her head forward, suddenly, and then her shoulders, first one and then the other and then, with a curious wriggle, alternates these movements, matching them with a jerky swinging of her extraordinarily suggestive but childish hips, first to one side, then to the other; soundlessly, yet as if there is, somewhere inside her, a pulsing music, an irresistible beat, a music to which the girl responds with a rhythm so full of intense feeling that the dance to this outwardly unheard music takes all her concentration and all her energy.

She is a thin girl. I'll tell you more about her later. She has only been in the school a few hours. Her father is something suddenly big in cooking oils and heavy haulage road transport. He knows he is not *comme il faut*, he does not even know the phrase. Miss Thorne, with a wry twist to her mouth which passes for a smile, realizes that he knows and accepts what he is but for his daughter he wants the polish.

"She needs all the spit and polish she can get," he leans forward in the large chintzy armchair.

"Spitting is not necessary, Mr Frome, and here, at Pine Heights, we do not encourage it," Miss Thorne says, "but polishing, that is quite a different matter." Getting up easily from her desk she draws aside the heavy curtain.

"The gels," she says graciously, "are having their bra burning ceremony this evening. Would you like to stay? We have a guest room. There's the bonfire pile down there in the corner of our meadow." She indicates a scrubby corner of a bald paddock known with affectionate pride throughout the school as "our meadow".

"Er. No thanks! I'd better be pushing off, er, thanks all the same."

"It's not a compulsory event," Miss Thorne lets the curtain drop, "it's simply for those gels who wish it, and we only burn old ones you understand," Miss Thorne explains, leading the way to the door. "Matron checks them, ticks them orf as being suitable, and for every one burned, a fresh one is put on the bill. It works beautifully. They have a

2

system to help out those with all brand new underwear, you understand, a gel with two old ones . . . "

"Yes! Yes!" Mr Frome is not used to hearing about underclothes, especially from a lady like Miss Thorne.

"One year, the first I think it was," Miss Thorne smiles dreamily, "we all got rather carried away. Hurled everything on to the fire — stockings, singlets, petticoats, pantyhose, pants — one girl even burned her nightie. Tonight there will be toffee apples, absooty scrumptious, and a sing-song round the bonfire. You are very welcome to take part."

Often Miss Thorne, at the end of afternoon school, pauses to watch the girls dancing. She has never, in all her years of experience, seen a girl dance as Debbie Frome, the new girl, dances. She seems to give off a ferocious sensuality. Some of the girls do not dance. Gwendaline Manners, a large fair skinned girl who has been a boarder since she was eight years old, never dances. She looks as if she would like to but is too shy. She is overweight and very tall for her age and is very quiet. Miss Thorne has invited Gwenda to accompany her to Europe during the vacation in May. Though she has not mentioned this to Miss Edgely yet, she has told her lifelong friend and travelling companion, Miss Snowdon. Miss Snowdon is matron of the Queens Hospital and a constant visitor to Miss Thorne's apartment, which she shares with Miss Edgely, on the upper floor of the Boarding House.

Both Miss Snowdon and Miss Thorne have the same kind of figure; a portliness brought on by years of responsibility, plenty of money, comfortable accommodation and good meals. Both women have the education, the background and the capabilities required for their positions. Neither of them cares too deeply for other human beings and they are not dangerously touched or moved by the human predicament.

Miss Edgely shares some of the qualities but, by contrast, is small. She has no taste and far less money.

* * *

"Dotty! Dotty!" Miss Peabody heard her mother's muffled voice calling, "Dotty! Dotty!"

"Oh Blast! she wants her hot milk," Dorothy Peabody muttered to herself and she pushed the novelist's letter under the embroidered cover on her dressing table. She would hurry up, she thought, and come back to the letter, back to Miss Thorne and Miss Snowdon and Miss Edgely as quickly as possible.

As she lit the gas under the hateful little milk saucepan she let her mind wander pleasantly. Whatever would Miss Thorne do with Gwendaline Manners in Europe! What an idea to take a schoolgirl on an expensive holiday like that and to pay all the expenses! It was beyond Miss Peabody's experience to understand why Miss Thorne should do this. What would the girl's parents think? It seemed an impulsive thing for a woman in Miss Thorne's position to do.

The milk frothed all over the stove.

"Oh drat!"

"Dotty! Dotty!"

"Coming mother." Dorothy Peabody poured the milk into her mother's special cup. "Drat the stove!" She thought she had better wipe it clean at once.

"Drat! and Drat!"

"Dotty!"

"Coming. Coming mother."

All day long fussing through filing cabinets while surreptitiously nibbling biscuits and screwing up and throwing away countless typing errors, she looked forward impatiently to the evening and to the novelist's letters. Every time she reread the letters she found something fresh, something she had not noticed before.

Already her stocking and hanky drawer was full of the thick envelopes with their bright extravagant stamps. For, of course, the novelist replied by air mail. All this correspondence because of her timid letter sent some time ago:

Dear Diana Hopewell,

I am writing to say how much I enjoyed your book *Angels on Horseback*. I found it so moving and sad that I was unable to read the ending for a long time. All the same the story has given me great pleasure and a wish for more of your work. The beautiful young schoolgirls and their strange and wild riding lessons brought something exciting into my life. (Mother and I live very quietly here in Weybridge.) And, the loneliness and the harshness of the Australian countryside fitted so exactly with my own feelings . . .

Secretly Dorothy Peabody signed her letter and posted it to the publisher. She did not expect a reply.

While reading the novelist's first letter Dorothy seemed to see her, Diana, dismounting from her horse at sunset to open the gates leading to her property. The dry grass would be pink in the light of the setting sun, Dorothy thought, like in the novel, and perhaps the grass would sing too, monotonously in that lovely place.

In the surprise and pleasure of receiving a letter in answer to her own, she allowed herself, for some days, to think of the novelist. Always she thought of her in the act of dismounting from her horse. All the time at work, secretly, she enjoyed the luxury of returning, in her mind, to this handsome image.

Of course, though she, like the others, chattered and gossiped the whole day, she did not mention the novelist in the office. Miss Truscott and the other typists would never understand. A book, a literary work of art like *Angels on Horseback*, would be wasted on them. And she did not tell her mother about either the book or the letters. Her mother was unable to leave her room and this gave Dorothy a sort of privacy; though it was uncanny how her mother seemed to know what she was doing.

"Dotty! You haven't dusted the front room mantelpiece." And,

"Dotty! Move the tins forward! You're using the tinned soup in the wrong order."

If Dorothy needed the bathroom in the night and crept there as quietly as she could, invariably her mother called out, "Dotty! Don't forget to switch off the light!"

"Who are you writing to Dotty? Who?" she called across the landing almost as soon as Dorothy, in an entirely new experience of excitement, began to answer the first letter.

"Who are you writing? Dotty? Who?"

"No one mother! Just nothing mother. Just, er, tidying my hair clips. Coming mother. Coming!"

The invalid had to be helped on to the commode at night after her hot milk and when, at last, she fell asleep Dorothy was free to reread the letters and to quietly write her reply.

I work in a large office, she wrote, we keep the sales records. It's typing and filing I do mostly. Miss Truscott's ever so nice. She has her hair done Thursdays and she lets me go a bit early to get mine done. Then there's Mr Barrington, Mr Bains and Mr Feathers and ever so many senior staff, it's a really big business. I've been with the firm thirty-five years, Miss Peabody considered the last sentence and it seemed too revealing; she crossed it out and wrote, "for ever such a long time", in place of the thirty-five years.

I am so interested, the novelist wrote back quickly. And do you know, I love your handwriting. It excites me! Perhaps I should say I am in love with your handwriting.

The sentences plunged across the enormous sheets of paper. Dorothy was quite taken aback and, on the day of that letter, made a whole series of serious mistakes at work.

Images came one after the other. She saw the novelist, charmingly dressed, mounted on her horse and galloping, with passion and grace, alongside a fence made with round poles, like the one written about in the novel. The horse, in a few minutes, covered the full length of the long paddock and seemed to gallop straight towards Dorothy turning only at the last moment to a steady dignified trotting. Even the word "paddock" said far more than either "field" or "meadow". Thus occupied with the splendid horsewoman, Dorothy failed to notice that it was raining quite heavily as she walked from the station along the dark streets passing houses identical with her own. Though she had a plastic hood in her handbag, she forgot to put it on. Surprised, she stood for a few minutes in the dingy hall with water dripping through the dangling corkscrews of her ruined perm.

Are you in love? the novelist want to know. What sort of dresses do you wear? Please tell me all about yourself!

Timidly she began to write an answer. Her dresses had meaningless blobby patterns on them; sensible dresses for the office. She was always anxious when she bought a new dress in case it was noticed. She went up to London every day to work, a short sedate train journey and a short walk at either end. The routine never varied. How dull this was in her reply. The same journey back to Weybridge in the late afternoon. In winter and the spring it was dark on the way home, and dark when she left in the mornings.

As for being in love. She threw away several pages. I expect my emotions are all frozen over she wrote. She found that she could not describe her clothes to the novelist, it was like trying to write details about a dog and a cat to show by a written picture that they were different in appearance. Suddenly her clothes seemed indescribable. She did explain however that it worried her to have to choose clothes.

On the way home from the shops, she wrote, I keep thinking of the one I didn't buy and that's the one I keep thinking I should have.

Miss Peabody looked at her neat handwriting on the blue sheets of paper, blue ink, blue envelopes. It was true her handwriting was nice. She hid the novelist's letters carefully and she thought she would spend more time on her own handwriting, improving the loops perhaps.

"Love letters eh?" Mrs Brewer, who came in every day to

sit with Mrs Peabody for a few hours, would enjoy asking, "Love letters eh?" over the cut lunch, about Dorothy's love life. Everyone was expected to have a love life to relate in confidence. Dorothy had two variations depending on which kind of audience the question came from.

Making sandwiches for her mother and Mrs Brewer with tinned asparagus tips and a particularly tasteless cream cheese was simply one more thing to get through, as Dorothy put it in her thoughts, before she could give herself up to her letter reading and writing. It was with a kind of unaccustomed impatience that she pressed the triangles of soft white bread into a plastic box. Mrs Brewer would unpack them the next day and carry them cheerfully upstairs prepared to eat most of them herself.

The nights belonged to the novelist.

I live on the gentle slope of a narrow valley, she wrote. I live in a ring of trees, very old trees and tall, taller I suspect than your English trees. In between the bunched foliage of glittering narrow leaves there are spaces of sky. There is just such a clear space between the trees like a harbour in the sky directly above my house and my sheds.

Even while Dorothy was still clearing up the breadcrumbs in the kitchen she was thinking about this harbour and how Miss Hopewell would look for it returning on horseback from the long ride she would have taken to inspect her fence posts. It was one of the favourite parts of one of the letters.

Diana, she hardly dared to think of her by this name, but she boldly did think and she murmured the name as she folded the bread paper meticulously with her fingers held stiff, careful, to make neat folds. She put the folded paper away in the drawer where she kept bread papers.

Diana, the Goddess of the Hunt, would be a tall woman graceful and shapely about the neck and breast. She would wear tall riding boots.

When I see the sky harbour ahead, I know I am nearly at my place, Diana wrote.

How wonderful, Miss Peabody did not notice how cold her bedroom was; how wonderful to know the way home by the tree tops and the paths of sky between the tossing foliage. Dorothy did not have to navigate. It was so simple to walk from the station. She did not even need a bus. The closeness of the station was the reason why her father, all those years ago, had chosen to live there. In his life he had followed the same drab pattern which Dorothy followed now. Every day, at the same time, leaving the brown painted front door and the solid wooden gate, going up to Peabody's Footwear For Men And Boys and, at the same time, in the evenings returning to open the gate in its dusty privet hedge and then to open the brown front door into the dark hall of the house. The only difference being that Dorothy made countless typing errors at Fortress Enterprises and did not sell shoes to men and boys.

Dorothy thought she would look at the sky and learn how to see shapes of it between buildings. This could even be useful in London, to know the sky harbours of the city. Though she lived near all her life and went up every day, except Saturdays and Sundays, she knew it was not difficult to be lost in London.

Looking at the sky was probably easier on horseback. In the city, looking up made her neck ache and she bumped into people. In no time her hat and her spectacles were knocked crooked and several people had tripped, treading on her feet.

"Excuse me!"

"Ooops sorry!"

"Ever thought of lookin' where you're goin' ducks?"

"Have more water with it."

"Hey watch it lady, your umberella got me right in the orchestra stalls."

Little lines of pain deepened round her eyes. She had corns.

9

Scurrying to her place in the office she thought again of Diana. It would be evening over there. Diana would be dismounting from her horse in the sunset. Long shadows would lie across the house and the sheds. Dorothy, for a moment, thought of the possibilities of sheds. There must be astonishing things in sheds. There would be pleasure simply to stand in the doorway contemplating sacks of seed, sacks of poultry food, mysterious machinery and tools, things like mattocks and crow bars which could give a person superior strength.

Diana had written that darkness came quickly and with it a silence broken only, in summer, by the endless chirping and crackling of the cicadas and in the winter, by the croaking of innumerable frogs. Dorothy, at her typewriter, knew that Diana, after eating a roast shoulder of lamb, would get up, not worrying about the washing up, and move thoughtfully across the large room to her writing table.

Sometimes the letters were disjointed and the novelist sent only a fragment which Dorothy guessed would slip into place sooner or later, unless, of course, it was discarded. Writers did not always use everything they wrote, the novelist explained.

Dorothy wished she had the letters in her handbag so that she could take a quick look. She tried to remember the last thing about Miss Thorne but was interrupted by one of the juniors placing a large file beside her.

Miss Thorne, in the pines often looks back to solemn moments, the novelist's most recent letter needed attention.

Miss Thorne looks back to a solemn moment in the shower, in a newly built motel in a remote township in the wheat.

"Edgely's gorn for a walk," she says stripping off her nightdress, "so why don't we . . . "

"Oh Super! Prickles!" Miss Snowdon often adopts schoolgirl language when she is with Miss Thorne. (Normally Snowdon speaks in a kind of medical jargon and you will notice that she and Thorne say "gel" and "orf" instead of "girl" and "off", it's an affectation, but I don't think they are aware of this themselves. Excuse the brackets.)

"Oh Super! Prickles! A water fight! Oh rather! Come on! Race you!"

"This bathroom is very nicely tiled. Good strong jets of water too."

"Mmm yes. Erotic. Rather. My deah this is madness!"

"Madness! But do go on!"

"Let's have the water just a bit warmer. Ah! that's more like it. Oh wicked! Prickles! Shall I soap you?"

"Of course you may do that again. As often as you like. You exquisite naughty. Oh indecently exquisite."

"Prickles! This is Bigger than both of us!"

"We'd better hurry deah, I think Edgely might be coming back, it was only a little health walk, to settle her insides after being cramped up in the car. She's been drinking hot water. No deah! nothing in it. Just plain, for the insides . . . "

Miss Peabody in her airless and virginal bedroom tried to make sense out of the letter which was scrawled in red and blue ink. She tried to piece together something of the lives of Miss Thorne and Miss Snowdon. There was a lack of sequence and she realized she must take each letter as it came and hope that in the end she would reach some sort of understanding.

Miss Peabody did not touch alcohol but on on this occasion she had a little of her mother's medicinal brandy in a cup of hot milk. It was soothing. The water fight had disturbed rather.

Love scenes are familiar, even repetitive, if you pick them

out of context and read them all at once, the novelist ended her letter with a little lecture in green ink. But it is the circumstances, the going towards the love making and then the time afterwards, the thoughts, d'you see, and the feelings which make the scenes memorable. Love scenes should be a whole lot of things. They can even be ludicrous, I mean, there is something ridiculous isn't there about naked human bodies. Now, the novelist continued, tell me all about yourself. Have you a small straight brave back? And are you in love? Tell me about your love, for I am sure you are in love.

Miss Peabody, even with the two teaspoons of brandy in her milk, could not answer such intimate questions. It was exciting to be disturbed by the water fight, who ever heard of such a thing. She thought of the mess in the bathroom and then wondered if it was possible to have a water fight by oneself. And then, of course, in the motel, it was a shower. There was no shower in the Peabody house. The District Nurse washed mother in bed with a bowl and flannels and towels. Every once in a while a second nurse accompanied the usual one, and, together, they lifted Mrs Peabody into a hot bath while Dorothy changed the sheets on her mother's bed. This was usually done at the weekend when Dorothy vacuumed the house and dusted the shelves and hung out the rather dismal washing they produced between them.

It was exciting too to be asked about being in love. Though she glanced at herself quickly in the hall-stand mirror before leaving the house every morning she had never looked long and deeply at or into herself. She did not know what her back was like. She knew her muscles were slack, horribly so round the regions of the waist and the buttocks but then she was, as she put it, on the wrong side of fifty and sitting at a typewriter all day did not help. Her skin too, she had let that go, or perhaps it had gone of itself without anyone noticing. Her skin was soft and toneless and colourless.

She blushed at Diana Hopewell's last question and at the statement it carried. Sitting at her dressing table, her hair in rollers and a hair net, Miss Peabody began to write. She wrote several of the large size air mail pages describing how, at the end of a gruelling day of conference at Fortress Enterprises, Mr Bains would emerge from the sanctuary of the inner office, wink in her direction and, with a special jerk of his head and a raising of his dark eyebrows, he has especially thick and dark eyebrows in contrast to his silver grey hair, she explained, he would elaborately hold open the door for her and they would go out together followed by the furtive, silent and envious looks of the other typists. Sometimes young Mr Barrington came too and she stood cheekily between them breathing in their maleness in the lift. She herself had "Je Reviens" of Worth Paris dabbed on her wrists and behind the ears.

It never fails, she wrote, remembering Miss Truscott's fervent tribute to Worth one Christmas.

Fortress Enterprises patronized a tavern, she explained on a fresh page, The New Light, quite near, just on the corner of the street. On Friday evenings one whole section of the tavern was taken over by staff from Fortress.

Mr Bains was a very sensitive man, Miss Peabody wrote, he was married but his wife had never understood him. Miss Peabody put down her pen; all this was Miss Truscott's. Mr Bains was Miss Truscott's. They even spent the night together sometimes. Dorothy often heard him explaining in a tired voice on the telephone to Mrs Bains somewhere out near Box Hill in Surrey that he had to go unexpectedly to the Midlands for an executive meeting. They would leave the office together, Mr Bains and Miss Truscott. On these occasions Miss Truscott carried a little mulberry coloured overnight bag. They often stopped for drinks at the New Light and it was said by others who went there, Miss Peabody did not frequent the tavern, that Miss Truscott, letting herself go on those nights, was always drunk when she left the New

13

Light on Mr Bains' arm. Thinking about those mysterious nights Miss Peabody, knowing Mr Bains to have a kind smile, imagined how gently he would put the dizzy Miss Truscott to bed in some comfortable hotel near by. She tore up the blue sheets of paper; Miss Truscott owned Mr Bains.

Starting afresh with clean paper Miss Peabody wrote briefly her other version of what she called "her love life"; that her young man had been killed in the war before the complete blossoming of the romance which was to have been hers. The medals which should rightfully have been sent to her were grabbed by the young man's mother who had never really cared for him.

I still have nightmares, she wrote, about his beautiful and innocent young body being blown to bits on the battle field.

It was hard to wait in patience for the novelist's reply with poetic condolences about the spirit of bravery ever present in a lifetime of fidelity.

Every morning she hurried downstairs to see if a letter was on the mat in the hall. Days went by and no letter came, nothing was on the mat, not even a gas bill. Forgetting about the blown up young man, he was only in her mind briefly on occasions when she had to furnish a love affair, she reasoned sensibly that the novelist was probably busy. It was, after all, February, and though there was plenty of rain and slush from unsettled snow in England, Diana's farm was suffering from drought.

From earlier letters Miss Peabody knew that Diana was hand feeding the horses at the fence and that she was trying to keep her fruit trees alive with frequent small offerings of brackish water carried in paint tins. Poultry too, Diana had written once, were often too foolish to drink even when fresh water was available in little troughs at just the right height. It was probably that Diana was having to stand and spray the hens, Miss Peabody thought, hoping that water would fall into their trembling gasping beaks. And of course there were the riding lessons, the girls in the novel *Angels on*

Horseback were not entirely fictitious. The horses and the girls would take up Diana's valuable time.

Smiling brightly all day at the office and being endlessly patient with her mother every evening Miss Peabody began to suffer. She longed for a letter from Diana. She lay in bed shivering on the long bleak cold evenings after the bleak cold days. She withered. She made mistakes at work and could not concentrate.

Unable to go on waiting she wrote to the novelist just a short note asking about Dr Thorne and Gwendaline Manners. Did they leave for Europe or did Miss Thorne change her mind?

Yes they do go to Europe, the novelist replied in a letter which came quickly, and the schoolgirl too, but I am not up to that part yet. If you remember I sent a fragment some time ago, Miss Thorne and Miss Snowdon having a shower. At present the three of them, Thorne, Snowdon and Edgely, are having a three day break driving through the wheat belt. Naturally Gwendaline is not with them; the shower part fits in on this trip. I do not always write everything in the order in which things appear in a finished book. There is too a thin line between truth and fiction and there are moments in the writing of fantasy and imagination where truth is suddenly revealed.

Miss Peabody felt warm again, she glowed somewhere inside herself; here was a wonderful letter. She was reading too quickly, she would go back and reread slowly.

Perhaps it is in writing, the novelist wrote, that the writer remakes himself and his world.

The three unmade beds in the motel unit have a curious effect on the women.

Their three day holiday is short in time but long in distance. Distances here are tremendous, the novelist explained. They drive all day in a small car to get to a remote tourist attraction in the eastern wheat country only a few kilometres from the rabbit proof fence.

Starving emus race or plod, depending on their state of starvation, up and down on the other side of this fence till they drop. Not a pretty sight. The emus are incidental, they are not the tourist attraction. People travel to this place to see some extraordinary rocks and caves.

There is a certain tension during the journey. It is a hot day and the sun is pouring in to the car. Miss Thorne is driving, Miss Snowdon is wedged in the other front seat and Miss Edgely is in the back. The luggage takes up most of the room.

They are late setting off as Edgely was not ready. She was and still is upset by something Miss Thorne said the night before.

"Prickles deah?"

"Yes Snow?"

"I know you don't, when you are driving, like to stop *en route* but what say you to a little light nourishment at the next road house?"

"Oh Rather! What d'you say Edge?" Miss Thorne is a little too hearty.

Miss Edgely's round blue-grey head is rolling and bumping from side to side with a regularity which reminds Miss Thorne of Edgely's repetitive stupidity at all times and which, in matters of the secretarial work at the school, is getting worse.

"Hey Dey! de li'l gal she 'sleep I tink," Miss Thorne, pressing her foot on the accelerator pretends to be a negress.

The uneasiness, mentioned earlier, felt on arrival by all three at the sight of the unmade beds in the room they are supposed to have, is linked to their uneasy experience in a dirty roadside cafe where they try to have some tea.

"Could we have a pot of tea for three please, and some toast? You'd like toast?"

Miss Snowdon and Miss Edgely say they would. Miss

Thorne smiles at the girl, who is waiting for the order.

"And some jam please," she says.

The girl stands with one hip jutting higher than the other; all the time she is glancing over her shoulder, through her long hair, to a little group of companions who are near the counter.

"No pots. Only cups. Black or white?"

"No pots? Three cups then please. Black thank you and sugar."

"Sugar's on the table," the girl does not return Miss Thorne's smile. She simply shifts her hips so that the other one is higher, as though resting the first.

"Oh yes. So it is! Toast, please, for three."

"There's only pies and up there on the board tells you what there is."

The three women glance up at the chalked scrawl.

"Oh, I don't think I really want a bucket of chips or a crayfish — it might not be perfectly fresh out here." Miss Snowdon laughs, lowering her voice for the last part of her sentence.

"Have you, perhaps, a biscuit?" Miss Thorne asks.

"Just what's up there on the board," the girl, tossing her hair, exchanges looks with the little group who are now gathered at one of the sticky tables.

"Oh well, we'll just have the tea then thank you."

It is not a comfortable place for the three ladies to sip their tea. It is not the kind of place where it is possible to slip a little fortification into the beverage. Miss Thorne, self consciously, and it is not like her to be self conscious, tries to tap her foot in time to the terrible music. The music is worse than anything the girls listen to in their own sitting rooms at Pine Heights.

Dirty curtains obscure any view over the surrounding wheat paddocks. The young people seem to have made up their minds to stare at the travellers.

"Of course," Miss Thorne, disconcerted, lowers her voice

to Miss Snowdon, scalding her lips on the deceptively hot tea, "they have nowhere else to *be*. I mean *where* in this whole empty country have these young people got a place to go!" At the words "whole empty country" she makes a gesture with her free hand and sends Miss Edgely's paper beaker of steaming tea straight into her unready lap.

"Oh! My deah! I'm so terribly sorry!" Miss Thorne jumps up spilling more tea as her large hip catches the corner of the wobbling chrome and formica table. "Are you badly scalded deah? I mean down there it's . . . "

"I'm quite all right," Edgely snaps. She is embarrassed and irritated as well as scalded. Miss Thorne, quite rightly, thinks she is near tears.

The beat and the whip crack and the thin haunting voice singing "I feel love" fills the squalid little cafe as they get up to leave. The music disturbs Miss Thorne bringing back to her an event from which she has not regained balance. As they move towards the door there is a moment of confusion as to which of the three ladies shall go out first. Miss Thorne distinctly over-hears unpleasantly rude remarks. She is sure they are being secretly jeered at. The uncomfortable feeling lasts for the rest of the long drive, and it is in this same frame of mind that all three of them survey with dismay the three unmade beds in the motel room.

It is a dark room, newly built and heavily curtained against known heat. The rubbish of leftover food has not been removed. The only sounds are the buzzing of enormous flies and the harsh voices of crows in the distance. The harvested paddocks stretch from the dusty piece of ground where the motel is to the horizon. Sheep are feeding on the wheat stubble. They move slowly, keeping together and spreading out towards the sky. A thunderstorm shower falling in one place, has left the sheep and the wheat stalks looking stained and patched.

The unmade beds cause private thoughts of hitherto

unknown erotic adventures to race and surge within the indignant breast.

"Men!" Miss Thorne says turning away in disgust. "I've no use for them, especially the sort who go on agricultural outings." She indicates the decorated mini-bus parked near by.

"Why isn't our room ready for us?" Miss Snowdon demands. They watch the men entering the swing doors leading to the office.

"Any way *à propos* . . . " Miss Snowdon jerks her head in the direction of the little file of male guests. "They're half your age deah, all except the one at the end, and he looks American."

"There must be another room," Miss Thorne chooses to ignore Miss Snowdon's remark which is in very poor taste, "if this room has been . . . er . . . used by three men it must be thoroughly cleaned out."

It is after this, when they are settled in a cleaner, if not perfectly clean unit, that Edgely goes off for her walk, the novelist explained. For the whole of the long car ride she has been brooding on the awful thing Miss Thorne said the night before.

"Your mother's a lovely woman," Mrs Brewer, the Peabodys' next door neighbour, often said this to Miss Peabody in a way which made Miss Peabody seem unlovely. Mrs Brewer, not having lost the use of her legs on the death of Mr Brewer, came in every day to sit with Mrs Peabody and to eat the fish paste or cream cheese and tinned asparagus sandwiches which Dorothy prepared for them. Mrs Brewer often referred to Dorothy's childhood, not having any children herself and therefore beyond criticism, in a thinly veiled critical way. There was often a hint in the tone of her voice that Amy and Mr Peabody had spoiled Miss Peabody,

"That child never wanted for anything Amy," Mrs Brewer accused and Mrs Peabody smiled her vague, sweet smile,

"We tried to do our best for her Nadine," she said.

Both women, widowed for almost twenty years, lived a great deal on events remembered or concocted. Through the hitched up curtain of the front bedroom window, Mrs Brewer entered watchfully into the various lives up and down Kingston Street bringing tendentious details to the notice of Mrs Peabody who sat, in brushed nylon, propped up on five pillows.

Miss Peabody in the lasting pleasure of the new letter took a hot bath. It was not her night for a bath.

"I'm a little prairie flower," she sang in the steam.

"Growing wilder every hour — flower — hour —

Nobody cares to cultivate me — mee — mee — mee

So-o I'm as wild as wild can bee — bee — be," she sang. It was the motel shower and the water fight which made her feel like a bath. Reading about food had the same effect on her. A description in a book of someone chewing a crisp apple, for example, immediately made her wish for one.

"I'm a little prairie flower," she sang and used up all the hot water.

Being liberated was what people called it now. In the office there was quite a lot of talk about liberation.

"Dotty! Dotty!" her mother called and called. "Are you ill Dotty?" Dorothy Peabody coming out of the bathroom heard the distress in her mother's voice.

"Dotty! Oh Dotty, oh my head! Dotty." She, unaccustomed to hearing the bath water so late at night and on the wrong night too, was sure Dorothy was ill. Not realizing that her daughter was singing, she thought the sounds coming from the bathroom were screams.

It took some time to soothe the old lady. Dorothy, happy with her letter and the late, out of turn, bath, remembered her own childhood earache and she remembered her mother's gentle hands, hovering in candlelight, putting something warm in her ear. It was somehow softening to remember this; it made it easy not to be impatient however selfish and tiresome her mother might be now.

They always read to her at night, one or the other, father or mother, sitting sometimes for hours in the cold bedroom when she had an earache or some other pain, reading from *Every Day Stories To Tell To Children* and Hans Andersen's *Fairy Tales*. Her room held within its dusty magic in those days images which returned and returned; the water closing over the ugly duckling; Tom, the tired little chimney sweep, making his way over Harthover and down Lewthwaite Crag, and on asking for water, the old Dame told him,

"Water's bad for thee; I'll give thee milk." Then there was Queen Telephassa who threw away her crown because it chafed her forehead; and, in particular, there were the pleasing preparations for physical comfort and security in *Robinson Crusoe*; and again, the wretchedness of Jane Eyre, cold and hungry at Lowood School.

Miss Peabody's father loved Dickens.

No one ever spoke to her now about Dickens or about Charlotte Brontë or Nathaniel Hawthorne or Defoe and gradually these things had slipped from her mind which became more and more the receptacle for office gossip.

Miss Peabody had not had an unhappy childhood. Her father, in spare moments, made things for her. He made, from a margarine tub, a toy box with a lid. It stood under the dresser. In it Miss Peabody kept all kinds of treasures, puzzles and coloured beads, little painted wooden dolls, a spinning top, crayons and glitter-wax. He made a dolls' house too, it was painted with bright colours; even pink roses were painted round the little front door. The dolls' house often stood, in winter, invitingly opened, in the warmest corner of the sitting room. Miss Peabody dusted and polished the little rooms and the tiny furniture every week and, when she was grown up and no longer had the dolls' house, she vacuumed and polished number 38 Kingston Avenue every weekend.

All the dancing lessons and the piano lessons and the birthday parties simply led Dorothy Peabody through the years, one after the other, from childhood to adolescence and, right under her mother's hopeful eyes, she turned into an old maid.

Mrs Peabody and Mrs Brewer were never able to understand it.

"She was quite a pretty little thing Amy," Mrs Brewer often said late in the afternoon as she prepared to gather up her things before going downstairs, "Funny thing really Mr Right not ever turning up." And Mrs Peabody would give a helpless little shrug and look up sadly at Mrs Brewer who stood tall beside the bed. Mrs Brewer always left at the same time every afternoon. The conversation, part of the ritual of farewell, lengthened the moment of leave taking. Mrs Brewer, leaving promptly, appeared to linger and Mrs Peabody had the chance, as Mrs Brewer thought of it, "to go down memory lane poor thing".

"She had such ducky party dresses too," Mrs Brewer sighed. "I'll never forget the little blue and pink embroidered reversible silk." Mrs Peabody remembered it too; a stupid little smile lit up her faded face.

"She should be here soon. Dotty should be home inside the hour," she said to her friend, "you go on home now, Nadine, you run along, you've got a lot to do. I'll be as right as rain now. Thank you for coming in, you are a dear!"

Mrs Brewer said, "Well, if you're sure now," and taking her various garments and sewing bags she would hurry away home to watch television and have something on a tray.

Sometimes it took Dorothy a great deal of time to soothe her mother.

"Do you remember, Dotty, the Christmas party when you had a lovely new frock with embroidered pink and blue flowers? And ribbons? Pink one side and blue the other?"

Yes, Dorothy remembered. "Well then what about the

22

dress mother? What about the party?" She tried not to be impatient.

"Well Dotty we had a little difference of opinion I think you must have been ten."

"Nine mother, I think." Dorothy set her mouth. She knew the time of soothing was going to be long.

"Well Dotty it was cold and I was afraid you would catch cold and you wouldn't wear your panties and you tore them up . . . "

"Yes yes mother I remember." Dorothy did remember the enormous baggy knickers which showed under the party dress. She remembered the scene or parts of it. She could have been a little girl again, remembering now so clearly. When her father, returning from the shoe shop, entered the living room he stood, perplexed, looking from Dorothy to her mother and at the two armchairs, one on either side of the fireplace, decorated with curiously shaped antimacassars of white fleecy lined cotton.

Dorothy Peabody, in the long enforced wakefulness, was tempted, for her own pleasure, to read the novelist's letters aloud to her mother, simply to be able to enjoy them all over again herself. Wisely she left them under her hankies and read instead the first chapter from *Great Expectations*. She read a second time the part where the convict turns Pip upside down:

The man, after looking at me for a moment, turned me upside down, and emptied my pockets. There was nothing in them but a piece of bread. When the church came to itself — for he was so sudden and strong that he made it go head over heels before me, and I saw the steeple under my feet — when the church came to itself, I say, I was seated on a high tombstone, trembling, while he ate the bread ravenously.

"Dotty!" her mother's tired little voice persisted, "there's an article on 'hair care' in the magazine over there on the dressing table." Wearily, Dorothy read about hair care.

As if in reward for her patience during the night, quite unexpectedly a letter from the novelist was lying on the hall mat when she made her way downstairs the next morning. Another letter, so soon, she could hardly believe it. She held the letter close as if embracing it. She had to rush to be on time for her train. She had, as usual, to stand for the whole journey and, because of being rushed all day she had to keep the letter, a thick one, till there was time and privacy to enjoy the reading. At last the tedium of the evening, the sandwiches for her mother and Mrs Brewer and the preparation of the hot milk, everything was finished and, in the chilly quietness of the bedroom, the novelist took over the night.

Edgely does not come across to dinner. Suddenly there is a silence, the dining room is dark, the generators have failed, the novelist's words flew over the page. Miss Thorne and Miss Snowdon after their shower are early in the dining room, they are the first people there and have been served with pork cutlets and some undefinable vegetables.

"Edge must be back by now," Miss Snowdon says, peering at the luminous hands of her wrist watch, "she's probably tired and is having a little lie down."

"I'm not so sure," Miss Thorne is anxious about her personal secretary, who is also a friend after all. She has not told Miss Snowdon anything about the stormy scene during the packing when they were getting ready to leave.

"Eat up Prickles!" Miss Snowdon puts a generous forkful of apple sauce into her own mouth. The agricultural outing men, coming in late, take their places in candlelight quickly provided, at a long table. Since all cooking has come to a halt temporarily they order wines. Several carafes are brought to them. They drink and, without food, are noisier every minute.

"Yes, that one must be an American," Miss Thorne with

disapproval peers through the gloom of the candle lit room. The two ladies are clean and rested, tranquil now because of the cleaner motel room. The hot meal is not so bad. They chew in comfortable rhythm, used to each other's mealtime habits.

"The thing about Edgely is that . . . well it's . . . " Miss Thorne pauses.

"Oh come on Prickles! She's tired that's all. She's probably had her brandy and has decided to miss din dins."

"It's like this Snow," Miss Thorne moves her food about adding some spinach-like substance to a sort of little rubbish heap on the side of her plate. "Edgely only just keeps her end up with us . . ."

"Oh Prickles! The mind boggles!"

"No, I don't mean that end deah. I mean the intellect not the physical. You know what I mean. That's why she always changes the subject so quickly all the time. You know her 'don't you think', her little phrase of change, it irritates me frantically but I put up with it, well, because she can't sustain anything for long, I mean," she adds hastily, "conversation and all that. For example, the other day when we were discussing *Othello* and the destructive force of jealousy, the unreasonable fury of jealousy, she chipped in changing the subject with some perfectly footling thing — a lost dog or something — brightly interposing her regular 'don't you think' all the time. She's always like that. She thinks she gives an appearance of intelligence with these irrelevant references to remotely associated ideas, you know, picking up from the conversation one word or phrase which could and often does belong in some entirely different context."

"Prickles Deah! So much from so little wine," Miss Snowdon says in a low voice.

Miss Thorne knows she is saying a whole lot of unnecessary things to avoid going back, in her mind, over the distressing scene after supper the night before.

"*Au fond*, Snow, I know I am in the wrong. I was very

clumsy with Edge when we were packing late last night," Miss Thorne tells Miss Snowdon.

"It was like this, we were sorting out clothes and things. 'Look Edgely,' I said to her, 'Edge I must tell you . . . ' I told her," Miss Thorne chokes on a breadcrumb and recovers, "I told her, 'You take the brandy Edge and I'll take the whisky.' We discussed our clothes, walking shoes, and so on. I said I was taking my tweed suit. I reminded her that it gets cold in the wheat at night, even when it's terribly hot during the day . . . "

"I can't see that that should upset her," Miss Snowdon says.

"Well no, it wasn't that. I told her, d'you see, that I have invited Gwendaline Manners to Europe, to accompany us to Europe when we go in May. She needs a change, a holiday, I'll explain about that later. I told Edgely I couldn't leave her all alone in school. The gel hasn't received a single invitation for any part of the vacation. It's not convenient to leave her at school. I can't take Bales and Mrs Bales orf board wages simply for one gel staying in school. Edge said a whole lot of things about big sixteen year old gels. I told her to take it easy. 'Edge,' I said, 'take it easy. Edge you're drunk!' I thought she would smash the brandy. I realized she wouldn't get orf to sleep. We had a terrible night, Snow. Edge was going on and on about the wine houses at Grinzing. I told her I knew we had to, in the presence of one of the gels, to uphold the honour of Pine Heights. I told her we'd go to Grinzing, that I'd arrange everything. I promised her that the gel would not make any difference to our plans. I promised her Grinzing. She all but smashed the place up," Miss Thorne cleans her nose vigorously, a nervous habit which Miss Snowdon cannot quite put up with in her friend.

"But Prickles deah, Edgely is quite right," Miss Snowdon looks away from the nose. "What on earth will you do with the gel when we all meet up in Vienna. I mean it's hardly a young gel's programme is it . . . Yes please," she turns to the young waitress who, for the evening, has squeezed her childish hips into some tight white jeans, "I'll have the chocolate mousse. What about you Prickles? I see there's an Apple Charlotte too, so difficult to make up one's mind! Now, I mean how on earth will you work out the accommodation. I can see exactly why Edgely's so upset, Prickles. She's probably hopelessly jealous. Where are the parents of this Gwendaline? Surely, it is their duty to remove her from school in the vac." Miss Snowdon makes short work of the mousse.

"That's just it Snow," Miss Thorne moves the Apple Charlotte with the tip of her spoon. "Gwenda's been in the school as a boarder for eight years. Her mother died when she was ten and since then she has been very close to her father. Last year he met a woman, a Mexican or something like it and, well, he's orf somewhere or other and married to this woman."

Miss Snowdon nods and Miss Thorne knows she does not need to explain more.

"The gel's very quiet. She will not be a nuisance I assure you. I tried to tell Edgely without much success. I mean she knows all about the gel, but it was impossible to break it to her about Munich and Vienna. I mean, the whole thing's only about fifteen days . . . " Miss Thorne is silent. In spite of all the trouble with Miss Edgely she is rather looking forward to the initiation of Gwenda into the art of travelling; the choosing of elegant clothes and how to wear them; and to the music and the art and the culture of Europe. After eight years at Pine Heights Gwenda is more than ready for a little finishing and what better way to attain it than to travel with her Headmistress; a kind of short pilgrimage to bring out in the gel a true appreciation of beauty in all its forms. All the same, Miss Thorne, in spite of the promised pleasure of introducing Gwenda to the opera, is not at ease in her mind about the vacation and the way in which she is really, by inviting Gwenda, upsetting all their usual arrangements.

Furthermore as she eats the clove scented apples and cream she suddenly feels worried about Miss Edgely. There is the possibility that she will not be safely in the motel room when they go back there after their leisurely and prolonged dinner.

The department of agriculture travellers, still waiting for their meal, are noisier and Miss Thorne knows that her tired nerves cannot stand much more. The idea of the short break had been to restore herself. She needs a rest, she tells herself, but if Edgely is upset then no one can have any kind of rest.

"The coffee's revolting Snow," Miss Thorne smokes one of her thin black cigars, "I think we had better go over and see if Edgely . . . "

"Good idea! It must be the water," Miss Snowdon pushes aside her cup, "It's undrinkable. Let's go over and have a brandy."

They slowly make their way across the sandy waste in the dark. The generators, which have started again, are rattling monotonously in the tin shed up against the back of the hotel a few hundred yards from the rough brick walls of the new motel units.

"I'm afraid Edgely's horribly upset," Miss Thorne says, "she's in the dark," she opens the door and switches on the light. "My God! you see, she's not heah!" Quickly they look in the bathroom and then at each other. Outside is the black night, there are no houses with lighted windows. The wind, as it always does at night, is rushing across the sheep trodden paddocks. It is bitterly cold. That Miss Edgely is still out on her walk is hardly credible.

"She must be lorst the poor deah!"

"We'd better wrap up and go and look for her!"

"Edgely not being intellectual at all, you know, is rather physical," Miss Thorne confides to Miss Snowdon in the car. They drive slowly down the winding road away from the black wind-rushed paddocks to the reserve. In the headlights the bush is grotesque and motionless. Trees, branches, leaves, undergrowth, even the road itself, all are sinister and as if waiting for something.

"I can't believe she's out here," Miss Thorne flashes her torch along the dust path which leads off between the moaning sheoaks. The trees, brittle with long drought, creak and sway, lifting and bending in the night wind which seeks out this place too. Miss Thorne shivers.

"How cold it is and how ugly!" she thinks.

The ground beneath their heavy feet resounds as if only a thin crust separates them from a hollow, perhaps horrible world beneath. The earth, as their feet plod and thud, squeaks and springs.

"Is it safe to walk here?" Miss Snowdon asks. She is, in spite of her solid safe body, frightened.

"Come on Snow! She must be somewhere out on the rock. Edgely! Edgely!" Miss Thorne's voice is thin. "Damn this blasted wind! Edgely! Edgely!" she calls, the note of irritation is mixed with fear in her voice.

"Edgely! Edgely! Where are you!" Still there is no answer and they continue along an endless path, they know it is endless having been down it before, between spiked bushes with black arms held out like the arms of starving people.

"Edgely!" Only the wind, moaning, replies.

"I feel some evil rites were performed here long ago," Miss Snowdon whispers but Miss Thorne, ahead, does not hear.

The cold is penetrating their thick coats.

Suddenly because of a stillness and a more intense cold they are aware that the tremendous rock formation is before and above them. The song of the wind changes; it seems to contain the voices of people talking, it swells and softens, it shrieks and laughs and disappears leaving a silence so empty that both women clutch each other.

"She can't have come this far." Miss Snowdon says hardly daring to speak. "She would be too afraid."

"The awful thing is Snow," Miss Thorne replies, "the awful thing is she might have walked this far and not noticed the time and then, in the dark, she will have got herself into a state . . . I mean, you remember what the place is like, we walked all round here once, last year wasn't it. Very different in sunshine and with campers and people . . . But in the dark, well she wouldn't know which way . . . "

"There's a reservoir on the top," Miss Snowdon reminds Miss Thorne.

"I know, I know, but she wouldn't go up there. Surely!"

The thought of the water brings a fresh feeling of dread. An immensity of water, an unknown quantity of water held in restraint. A power of water and a weight of water above them collected on the concave tops of the rock and held there in specially constructed walls.

It is easy to imagine the icy depths of this water and easy to think too how it could roar down the rock face if a break in the wall occurred.

Miss Thorne flashes her torch. They are face to face with the smooth rock. The two women's heads ache with the cold.

"I don't think she could be here," Miss Snowdon's teeth are chattering. She can hardly speak.

"She must be!" Miss Thorne flashes her torch.

"Oh! don't flash it upwards I can't bear . . . "

"We'll have to go along the foot of the rock, there's a path."

Of course other people could be out visiting the rock by night. There is a place for camping quite close. Miss Thorne can, in spite of the horror of the night, imagine how wonderful it would be to set up camp in the dark, especially if one brought someone, a friend, who was not familiar with the place, and to sleep curled up in the warmth of a sleeping bag, with other people curled up in theirs and then to wake early, just at dawn, to see the rock curving upwards, towering into the sky as if it had arrived at some time during the sleep of humans. Miss Thorne has a liking for introducing people to fresh exciting experience. It is however not the time of year when many people choose to go on a camping holiday. It is unlikely that there are any people near.

"There's no one here at all," Miss Snowdon whispers, "we'd better go back to the car."

"Yes, she might have gorn in the othah direction," Miss Thorne gives a few final flashes with her torch in all directions, including the grim rock face.

"Look! Look! There's someone there! over there!"

"Where?"

"There! Just along there only I don't think it's Edge."

"It might be a rock or a bit of scrub. Oh, I daren't look."

"We'll have to."

"What, what if it isn't her!"

"Edgely!"

"Edge old gel! What do you think you're doing!"

"Oh Edgely, we've been so worried. Quick, come back to the car at once. You're frozen! We're all freezing! Hurry! Hurry!"

Together they haul the stupid woman back to the place where the car is and bundle her into the back seat. Miss Thorne, thoroughly chilled, is angry. She only just restrains herself from instantly breaking both Miss Edgely's legs and twisting her silly head off. How much simpler life would be without her, she reflects. Probably her head would only half twist off and that would not do at all. It is some consolation to remember that, between them, they nearly ran Edgely off her bandy wooden-doll legs and that her head jolted from side to side as they ran.

"I tried to die but I couldn't," Miss Edgely, relieved at being found, is her bright self. "I just couldn't die!" she seems pleased with the idea and keeps on repeating it.

Miss Thorne, her mouth shut in a line, does not say anything. She wants to be first into a hot shower and straight into bed with a double Scotch. Ungraciously she will insist that Miss Edgely and Miss Snowdon take their showers first.

She prays, without their knowing, that there will be enough hot water at the inefficient motel.

While Miss Snowdon is in the bathroom, Miss Edgely, who is in her nightdress, suddenly starts to howl,

"It's all right for you Ella. You've got everything going for you. Everything's sewn up for you. You've got it all your way. You've got your school and your position. You're a sort of Goddess Ella. You can do or get anything you've got a mind to do or get. It's different for me, I've only got you in the whole world."

Miss Thorne, who is still cold, not having had her turn in the shower, is horrified.

"Edgely don't!" she begs. "Please don't. Don't cry! We've all had a bad fright. Now don't cry! Look Edge, Snow will hear you — and those men, you know the agriculture men, they will hear you, they're next door to us, they will hear all along the units if you make such a row. Edgely!" Miss Thorne tries to console Miss Edgely. She pats her and strokes her awkwardly.

"There, there, Edge! It'll be all right." She can never handle Miss Edgely in tears because tears demand the physical caress.

Miss Thorne feels guilty in spite of being intelligent enough to know that Miss Edgely is being entirely unreasonable. After all here she is having the privilege, as she always does, of being away for a few days' holiday with Miss Snowdon and herself.

It is Miss Snowdon in her sensible navy blue dressing gown who quietens Miss Edgely and helps her into bed, tucking her in gently as if she was a patient.

"What will you do, Prickles, with the schoolgirl in Vienna?" Miss Snowdon asks carelessly, in the dark, when all three are in bed. "I mean our own programme is hardly suitable is it for a schoolgirl?"

"Oh! ship her orf back to school," Miss Thorne replies in a bored voice. She is still sitting up in bed with a double Scotch in each hand and two spares lined up on the bedside table.

But Miss Edgely, for whom the conversation is intended, without the intellect to stay awake when physically comforted, is fast asleep after her heavy day.

The structure of my story, the novelist wrote to Dorothy Peabody, is so complicated that, in my notes, I have to use different colours, you know, green ink to remind me of what Edgely is doing, red for Thorne and blue for Snowdon. I have even got some pieces of coloured paper to write on to help me when I am sorting out the different incidents. To give you an idea of Thorne's absolute dedication to her school, she has written a school song with the words Pine Heights on top G at the end of every stanza. There are ten stanzas. She has a moment of exquisite pleasure one morning when the girls are singing and, on the top G, a window shatters in the gymnasium. Inside herself she is very proud of her song and the rewarding sound of the breaking glass is something she will never forget. She is very modest about the song and goes out quietly to find Bales, the outside man.

"Bales," she says, "our song this morning broke the end window in the gym," she is very calm, "please will you put in some fresh glass."

Bales does not tell Miss Thorne that it was his grandson throwing rocks at his grandmother. Incidentally, in parenthesis, though this will not be in the novel itself, it is not irrelevant to say here that Mrs Bales does the kitchen for Miss Thorne. This is just one of those details which is absolutely necessary for the writer to know but which does not always reach the reader.

I think Thorne is selfishly enjoying the prospect of Gwendaline in Europe and Edgely, perceiving this, is madly jealous. For all Edgely being insignificant and small brained she does have her human feelings and needs and, in the novel, these must be respected. After all Thorne obviously has been the one to take Edgely to Europe on previous occasions. Edgely's delight, even if simulated, at being introduced to incomprehensible paintings and to the difficulties of unaccustomed opera, will have excited and pleased Thorne at one time. It is a tremendous pleasure to initiate a person whom one believes to be innocent.

To be the initiator . . .

Miss Peabody had to stop reading the letter. She clasped it to the front of her blouse. It was *Angels on Horseback* all over again and yet excitingly different.

"Dotty! Dotty!" her mother was calling.

It was hard to put aside Diana Hopewell's letter. The letters were coming quite fast. In the mornings now there was often a letter lying on the hall mat. The drawer was stuffed with them. Miss Peabody thought that one quiet night she would sort them into order and number them. She looked forward to doing this very pleasant work. She thought it would be nice to buy some ribbon and tie the letters into "easy to handle" bundles. She would label them, "The personal letters of —

"Dotty!"

"Coming mother," Miss Peabody's voice was melodious. In her pleasure, looking forward to the rest of the new letter, she hardly noticed all that had to be done down in the kitchen and up in her mother's bedroom.

"Milk O! Mother Milky O Mother!" she sang.

"Dotty are you ill! What's that noise?"

"Nothing mother." She poured the warm milk quickly down her mother's astonished throat and had her out on the commode and back into bed before her mother could utter another "Dotty!"

"Our Father which art in Heaven Hallowed be Thy Name Amen Goodnight mother amen mother."

"Dotty! You're not on your knees!"

Miss Peabody, suddenly seeing the expression on her

34

mother's face, without remembering Diana Hopewell's words about respecting human feelings and needs (she was unable to remember anything for long), bent down and kissed her mother's bewildered face. Then, kneeling down as usual, she said The Lord's Prayer softly and sweetly adding a part of the twenty-third psalm which brought to her mind images of Diana's farm which was, she was sure, used as landscape and setting in *Angels on Horseback*.

"In pastures green . . . " Lovely word pasture.

"Oh Dotty! thank you so very much," her mother looked comfortable.

"Good night mother."

"Good night Dotty."

Miss Peabody, in her nightdress, continued to read the letter. The pages had an exotic smell, a perfume of spice was it? A sweetness as of strange pleasures to be had from smoking wild herbs and specially prepared roots. A fragrance belonging to good food and wines.

The reason for Thorne being so tired, the novelist wrote, is not simply the preparation for the beginning of the new term. It is not the *Othello* lectures and the production of the play. Thorne loves literature and she revels in lecturing and she adores producing Shakespeare. She enjoys exciting hitherto unknown, as she thinks, passions in the breasts of young girls while remaining calm and dignified herself, in charge, as it were, of their passions. She watches, with pleasure, the feelings which begin to grow in the youthful girlish Othello, *All's well now sweeting; come away to bed*, and makes them rehearse the scene till eyes sparkle and cheeks are flushed.

The tiredness is something else, a mixture of things partly relating to Miss Edgely who is not handling her menopause at all well and is highly emotional and more unreliable and muddle-headed than usual; and partly to having, on an impulse, invited the shy, unsophisticated Gwendaline Manners to accompany them on the short holiday to Europe in May; and there is something else too, an unpleasantly disturbing little incident which took place soon after the beginning of the term.

As Headmistress Ella Thorne is used to all sorts of difficulties, hysterical girls, angry cooks, bullying or demented parents and inexperienced unqualified staff. It is not so much the actual incident; it is more what the incident implied and its continued implication.

One night, very late, Miss Thorne is in bed reading. In her hand, a heavy tumbler of Scotch. She is enjoying the energy and the majesty of the writing in *Rasselas*, rumbling phrases aloud to herself and hicupping from time to time. It does not suit her digestion to read in bed. ... *the spritely kid was bounding on the rocks, the subtle monkey frolicking in the trees, and the solemn elephant reposing in the shade.*

She reads and sips and rumbles and suddenly the Boarding House, on the same floor as her own house, resounds with music. The girls have music every day in their sitting room in the School House but this is at eleven thirty and everyone supposedly in bed and asleep. With the music, which is very loud, there is a remarkable rhythm and a penetrating beat; a girl with a thin mournful voice is singing; someone is dancing in the passage.

Miss Thorne sips her Scotch and waits. Matron is sure to be out there at once to silence whatever revolution is now taking place. Matron has been having her share of troubles; there having been a series of nocturnal raids on the staff supper table lately. It has taken a mustering of good manners to be able to sit down to the meagre leavings following the raids and not to complain, with disgust, at blancmanges and trifles which bear the signs of hands trying to grab what is best handled with a spoon. Miss Edgely, found by Matron on one occasion, has not been able to recall how she came to be bound and gagged and left in the pantry.

The music and the dancing continue so there is nothing to

do but go out there. There is a door from Miss Thorne's apartment directly through to the Boarding House.

The girl with the long fringe over her eyes is dancing. Her shoulders, angular in a spangled dress, move alternately with her moving hips as she moves along the wooden boards of the passage towards Miss Thorne who stands sturdily in her doorway. She is amazed at the spectacle. At the far end a group of excited girls in nightdresses and pyjamas are watching. They disappear silently in various directions as the enormous figure of the Headmistress advances slowly. The music beats on.

The girl Debbie, whatever her name is, Debbie Frome, is dancing with that strange internal ceaseless energy. She dances a few steps forwards a few steps backwards a few steps to one side a few steps to the other side her head nods and turns as her body moves forward in a jerky rhythm and a purposeful beat propelling the dancer forward two-three *and* back two-three *and* left two-three *and* right two-three *and* back two-three *and* forward *and* forward. She dances as if she does not know any one is there. Her expression is one of concentration and her whole body belongs in the fantastic rhythm. The uneven hem of her dress has seductive qualities.

"Turn orf that noise and send that gel to my room," Miss Thorne's voice rises above the music. "And see that she takes orf that frock."

She waits for Debbie Frome in her room. She has thrown some wood on to the dying fire, a little blaze is springing on the hearth. She sits making a few notes about *Othello* at her writing table.

"The irony of the play," she writes, "is that the audience know before Othello himself knows what is happening to him."

There is a knock on the door.

"Come in," Miss Thorne calls in her most musical voice. The girl, Debbie Frome, enters. For want of something to replace the immodest dress Matron has tied a domestic science apron tightly round the slender body.

Miss Thorne looks up, smiling, from her notes. Her dressing gown is crossed over and tied securely with a magnificient cord bearing two coloured fringed tassles. It is reminiscent of what Othello might have worn when celebrating his nuptials. Miss Thorne has already made a note to remember to lend the cord for the dress rehearsal.

"Come in to the fire, child," she says pointing to the armchair, a big chintzy thing which she does not like but which makes parents feel safe as does the wallpaper which is covered with pink cabbage roses.

"Would you like some hot milk?" she asks crossing graciously to the bell, forgetting there would be no one to answer at this late hour.

"Nope!" Debbie sits down crossing her legs one over the other, the stiff apron, cracking starch, pulled tight round her and slipping to one side to show her long straight strong legs.

"No?"

"Nah! I mean, no thank you."

"And what is the dance Debbie?"

"It's disco Miss Thorne, it's disco. Do you know disco? I'll show you disco. It's easy once you know how. Here! I'll show you." She stands up and starts to step forward two three, "I'll show you the camel kick huh?" She sings and dances:

"I don't know where you come from —
Heaven must have sent you/
You held my hand/ You held my hand/
When you needed me you needed me . . ."

"No. No thank you Debbie. I'm too old for that sort of thing." Miss Thorne smiles kindly. She's thinking that the apron suits the gel. The aprons should be used more often; there was something virginal and attractive about them especially when worn next to the skin like this. The gels would make the most of themselves in the aprons. Well, the ones like Debbie. Not Gwenda unfortunately.

"You're not too old. You're not too old Miss Thorne," Debbie dances up to her Headmistress, "I like you as you are," she sings. She dances round and round and Miss Thorne is obliged to turn and turn.

"Turn!" Debbie says. "Turn and turn and step but don't touch! Not yet!" She's laughing. "It's disco Miss Thorne. It's disco!" The girl is singing softly and dancing round and round her.

"Come on Miss Thorne, Miss Arabella Thorne, I can teach you. I can teach you a lot of things. I can teach you what to do with your hands."

The girl is close to the woman and as she dances she is even closer but does not touch.

"In disco there's no touching," she says, "you turn me on I'll have to come," she sings, looking up at her Headmistress through the ragged, long fringe of hair. Her eyes through the fringe have a teasing look in them. "Are you turned on Miss Thorne? You like this Miss Thorne Huh? Huh! Huh! Huh! Would you like to touch me now," she sings, dancing up and back, "Would you like to touch me now."

"No thank you Debbie," Miss Thorne replies quietly, looking down from her immense height. "And now I think it is time for bed," she looks at her watch. "Good gracious! it's well after midnight. What about our Beauty Sleep? Part of the night is for sleep, especially for you young gels with examinations ahead. So goodnight Debbie, orf you go now, orf into bed!"

"Miss Thorne, I want to stay with you all night. Can I stay please?"

"I am afraid that's not possible Debbie. I do however completely understand your feelings," Miss Thorne speaks kindly in a low voice, lowered on purpose in kindness and to hide any trembling in her voice. "Everyone has disturbed nights at some time or another Debbie. Sometimes it's homesickness, sometimes it's worry over school work, sometimes the disturbing feelings are sexual, but whatever the reason, it is now time for sleeping. And here at Pine Heights we all sleep in our own beds. Goodnight Debbie. Sleep Tight!"

The girl is sullen but goes towards the door.

"Goodnight Miss Thorne."

Miss Thorne, alone in her room, shyly but quickly admits to herself that she has been tempted. "What a delicious yet terrible thing temptation is," she says to herself, "especially for someone in my kind of position!" There is no one with whom she can discuss it. Slowly she paces up and down in front of her dying fire. For a moment she thinks how charming it would be to take young Debbie to Europe in place of Gwenda; but quite rightly she cannot do that. Gwenda is already invited.

The invitation was given about ten days earlier in the Visitors' Room. The girls see their personal visitors in this well polished room which is opposite Miss Thorne's office downstairs. Usually Matron is present or one of the junior mistresses, and if there is no junior mistress as sometimes happens during staff changes, then Miss Edgely presides. This time it is Miss Thorne herself as the visit is of a delicate nature.

"So my dear, you will have a new mother. I hope you will be kind to her as she is very young," Mr Manners is standing by the window not looking at his overweight daughter.

"Racquelle and I were married yesterday and we leave for Brazil tomorrow." He turns to Miss Thorne. "Business with diplomacy with pleasure," he gives a sunburned-grey-at-the-temples-flash-of-gold-in-the-back-teeth-smile in the direction of the Headmistress and, without wasting any of it, passes it on to big pale Gwenda.

"My firm is opening a branch in Brazil," he explains, "and Racquelle's family, with whom I have to come to some sort

of, how shall I put it, some sort of truce, are there too . . . "
He is tactful and does not dwell on his pleasure which is part
of the combination.

"Yes of course," Miss Thorne says.

Mr Manners looks at a cabinet which contains a display of
Edible Art by the Form V girls. On the polished table is a
wooden bowl of green apples, windfalls. Beside it is a notice
neatly typed by Miss Edgely:

SOME OF BEAUTIFUL FRUIT SERVED IN OUR DINNING HAIL.

Miss Thorne frowns slightly; it's always the same when
Edgely does anything in capitals, Errata! Errata!

Gwendaline's holiday at school is arranged swiftly with
the signing of a cheque and a present dropped lightly into
her ample lap. Mr Manners writes a second cheque as he
decides, on the spot, that Gwenda should spend the whole
year in school to enable Racquelle to become thoroughly
accustomed to her new position.

Miss Thorne, returning from the hall after the departure of
Mr Manners, is dismayed at the sight of the tears pouring
down the girl's white cheeks. Gwenda has not made any
attempt to get up from her chair.

"Now Gwenda," Miss Thorne is brisk, "you have been in
school before sometimes, haven't you, for the holidays and it
has not been all that bad. Come along Gwenda, that golden
wrapping paper will be ruined if you cry all over it. Come
along, deah, open your present!"

Unused to disobedience of any kind, she stands and
regards the constant welling and overflowing of the silent
tears for a few moments and then steps across the hall to the
office and asks Miss Edgely to have tea and toast sent in to
the Visitors' Room.

It is over the comfortable tea tray that Miss Thorne issues

her invitation. Gwenda, who has never travelled, shyly accepts.

Miss Thorne has put a match to the gas fire and the heat has caused her cheeks to be flushed. Even Gwenda's pale face is pink by the end of the afternoon. Together they munch their toast and discover that there is enough hot water to allow them two cups each.

Miss Thorne stops pacing to and fro in her room, the heavy tumbler needs replenishing. She eats a thick confiscated ham sandwich. Haunted still by the rhythm of the beat and the girl's dancing movements the idea of sleep is impossible. Of one thing she is certain, that Gwenda having been invited to accompany her to Europe means that this other girl, with her remarkable qualities, must be left behind. To put it plainly Debbie would steal the show. Miss Thorne does not even flinch at the cliché. "Either Gwenda comes alone or no one goes," Miss Thorne addresses her reflection in the mirror in her own bathroom. She tries a little quotation from *Othello*.

"Otellello . . . oh Good Heavens I've had Ah too much. Anyway this Debbie whatsaname may not Ah how shall I shay it Ah be shootable Hay Hay even to stay on at Pine Heights so why take her abroad,

" 'But jellied sholes will not be answered sho Otellello.' "

Miss Thorne, sitting up in bed in the dark motel room, works her way through the prepared fortifications of double Scotch. She is still fighting off the desire to break every bone in Miss Edgely's boring body. During the stupid woman's howling she uttered a few disquieting things,

"But you know perfectly well Ella, you know as well as I do, the girl's a thief. Oh Arabella how can you!"

"Yes, Yes, Edge, I know, but only once. She only stole

42

something once . . . now hush your noise do. Snow's coming out of the shower any minute."

Miss Thorne goes over the conversation though she would rather not.

"She stole from her room mate! I mean, how low can you go, I mean, she stole from a friend!"

"Yes, Edge, yes. I know, it's because she hasn't any friends, not real ones. She's lonely, that's why she stole. She's terribly lonely, Edgely."

"Well other people are lonely too," Miss Edgely has a fresh outburst of crying, "and to steal something even if its only a little money and some chocolate means she's capable of stealing. And, if she's with us it's likely she'll steal from us. She'll steal from you and she'll steal from me."

Stealing chocolate Miss Thorne thinks is so unbearably sad. And Edgely too, that's sad. Jealousy. Edgely is being so difficult. She listens to Edgely snoring.

But jealous souls will not be answered so;
They are not ever jealous for the cause,
But jealous for they are jealous: 'tis a monster
Begot upon itself, born on itself.

"Still busy in your head with work, Prickles? Othello?"

"Oh yes, sort of, Snow. Yes, Othello."

"Good night, when you're ready Prickles."

"Good night Snow."

The night in the wheat is the blackest kind of night.

"Half an hour in the mornings and half an hour in the evenings, not just a stroll but a good brisk walk," Miss Thorne remembers her doctor's advice and plunges through the pines. She has the idea that this would be good for the whole school.

"Not in the pines Edgely deah, Nature is too frail, once round the games field don't you think and down to the gates and back at the jog-jog-jog. Here is a memo for you to type out, there's a deah, let me see, perhaps three mornings a week, give it to Matron and ask her to put it up on the notice board."

Miss Thorne is encouraging culture in the school, music and drama and creative writing, the novelist, in starting her letter, neglected to mention the fact that Miss Peabody had been to the doctor with some palpitations and that he had given her tablets to take for the rest of her life.

"I've got Blood Pressure," Miss Peabody told the office staff proudly on the Monday morning.

"Hasn't every one?" Mr Bains, who was just passing through the main office, muttered.

Miss Peabody had written a full description of her visit to the doctor and how she was to notice how she felt when taking half a tablet and how she was with a whole tablet. It was a little disappointing that Diana made no answering remark in her letter about the blood pressure. For a few days it had seemed more important than anything but, as Miss Peabody began to devour the letter, her mind slipped off the matter.

Miss Thorne is encouraging culture in the school, music and drama and creative writing, the novelist wrote, at present she is introducing the mythology in small doses. She is hoping some of the girls will write poetry. And of course, there is the production of *Othello*.

Mr Minsk comes every day to give piano lessons. The school has its own orchestra. Miss Thorne herself plays the cello, Mr Minsk sits with his eyes closed listening, with carefully concealed horror, while Miss Thorne, her skirts drawn back, the cello grasped between her substantial thighs, practises. She practises alone mainly but, at times, is accompanied on the piano in the music room by Mr Minsk.

There are occasions when she joins the orchestra. She knows she plays badly and she is fully aware that Mr Minsk is trying to hide his agony. She loves the cello, it means a lot to her. She knows the girls in the school orchestra cannot

44

play either. All need each other even if all of them, unable to keep up, drag along at their own pace.

"Mr Minsk," Miss Thorne says, "I would so like the orchestra to tackle a Brandenburg Concerto even if it takes a week to get everyone through to the finishing line of just one movement."

"Yes of course Mees Torn if you say it." Mr Minsk gives his noble little bow.

"We could try and have it ready for performance during the Parents' weekend next term," Miss Thorne says with delighted enthusiasm.

Sometimes before taking her walk down through the fragrant pines Miss Thorne stops to listen to Mr Minsk playing the flute. It is his instrument. He plays for the students during their music lessons. He likes to do this, it is relaxing.

"Play for me Mr Minsk," a little girl, bored with the destruction of Chopin, asks. The girls like him to play because it means less time at the piano.

Mr Minsk is a Pole. His name is not Minsk at all but Miss Thorne thinks it is better to have a name which everyone can pronounce and spell.

She stays on by the door while the Aubergine twins, serious little girls with square cut hair and round spectacles, pound their way through their concert duet. They play on two pianos; Miss Thorne has arranged the music room to make this possible. One of the twins is learning something to accompany Mr Minsk's flute. Miss Thorne is very pleased about this. It is touching to see the young girl and the older man, a relationship which always excites the imagination, support each other and perform for each other. She enjoys the rapport so clearly established between the young piano player and the elderly flautist.

The regrettable thing is that Gwendaline Manners, so many years a boarder in the school which has so much to offer, simply has no instrument.

* * *

The novelist was sorry she had not written for some time. She was burning off her paddocks and ploughing fire breaks, three metres wide. The early rains had been welcome, she wrote, her dams were beginning to fill at last. It was heavenly to smell more rain in the wind.

Miss Peabody, who hated to get wet and had plastic squares and hoods in her handbag in readiness for the all too frequent rainy days, could not fully understand this pleasure in the rain. People who wanted rain, she thought, should live in England. She tried to imagine the hot dry Australian summer. She knew about it from *Angels on Horseback* because the novelist had written about the bald, dry earth resounding under the horses when the schoolgirls galloped by on their strange, erotic, nocturnal adventures.

She realized she really had no true idea of heat.

Do you travel much? the novelist wanted to know which places she preferred in Europe.

Miss Peabody travelled every day except Saturdays and Sundays up to London and back. She could write in her letter a description of the crowded trains and of the men in the First Class compartments, seen from the corridor, who always had their same seats and played cards during the repetitive journeys. Bridge was it? Some snobbish card game requiring intellectual skill rather than luck.

With her blue pen held over the blue paper Miss Peabody paused wondering what to write, remembering an excursion from school across the English Channel, years ago, from Dover to Calais.

The French mistress at school arranged it, she wrote. She described how she was sick all the way across.

A French sailor had given one of the girls an orange. At the time Dorothy Peabody, suffering at the rail of the steamer, did not care who had received an orange. Later at school the orange and the giver of it seemed to have special significance to the receiver and her immediate friends.

A sailor on the boat gave me an orange, Miss Peabody

wrote. Feeling at once unable to write this to the novelist, she wrote the truth saying she supposed there must be something wrong with her because no one had ever offered her an orange or anything else. She did remember a few other things about Calais, that it was raining all day for one thing; and that old women were sitting on the quay with baskets of cut flowers and apples to sell. They spat on the apples and polished them on their skirts and on their jacket sleeves. Dorothy had picked up an apple to buy one, but it must have been a misunderstanding, she wrote, because the old woman had given her hand a sharp slap and had snatched the apple away.

Miss Peabody, not happy with these carefully forgotten memories, stopped writing and looked at the novelist's letter again. On the last page was a flamboyant P.S.

Please excuse this violet ink, the novelist had written, I am trying out a different colour for Miss Thorne. I do not know if it will work.

I am trying to get another book of mine for you, it is out of print. It's only short, novella length, it's called *Love At Second Sight*. A very beautiful film is being made of it so the paperback cannot be released until the film is finished. The story itself is very simple, a bit sordid in places, it's about two utterly abject women, both post menopausal, who have a brief and unexciting love affair.

The affair lasts from Christmas till Easter and Easter is early that year. Afterwards they keep up a desultory friendship enlivened with occasional outbreaks of spite. The producer is tremendously excited about the whole thing, especially the setting which is mainly in a flat boring street in an incredibly dull suburb. One of the women early on in the story says,

"I can't see what you see in me," and the other replies,

"I can't either."

For the paperback edition I've had to practically rewrite the book and large chunks of it are devoted to the major wars and to the depression and to mass production, unemployment, computers, space travel, the nuclear weapon scene, drugs and, at the end, inflation so you see it's very topical. It will be serialized in our local newspaper.

Write quickly, the violet ink sprawled to the bottom of the page, and tell me all about yourself, your mother, Mrs Brewer and the old Blood Pressure how is it?

Miss Peabody gave a little gasp, Diana had mentioned the Blood Pressure after all; in her hasty first reading she had failed to notice the novelist's thoughtfulness. She went back to finish the page.

... meanwhile Miss Thorne, Miss Edgely and Gwendaline Manners are on their way to the Pension Eppelseimer in Vienna where they will be joined by Miss Snowdon who is, at the same time, journeying from Lucerne where she has been attending a conference on Family Health. At very short notice she had to step in over an unexpectedly dead colleague and deliver a paper on "The Forgotten Placenta, its identity in our Society".

— More in my next letter —

Dorothy Peabody crouched at her dressing table in the chill early summer evening listened to her mother's gentle snoring and wished for the morning and the door mat in the hall with a thick envelope on it decorated with expensive stamps.

Miss Thorne, Miss Edgely and Gwendaline Manners are safely in the express from Munich to Vienna, the novelist, without any details from her own life or any questions about Miss Peabody's, and without any apology for delay in writing, began her letter straight with her travellers.

They are tired after Munich. The long journey by train crossing the mountains and valleys of Central Austria is welcome. Miss Thorne sits smiling, comfortable in her window seat. Opposite, with her back to the engine, for she is young enough not to mind, is Gwenda. Miss Edgely, emulating Miss Thorne, has a seat facing the engine; that is, looking forward in the direction in which the train is travelling. Gwendaline is neatly dressed in her well brushed blue blazer; her school hat is sitting straight on top of her pale fair hair.

Gwenda, like Miss Thorne, looks out of the window. Mountains and more mountains come and go. Even from inside the train there is the feeling of knowing the exquisite sensations of the clear air outside. Miss Edgely has her eyes closed.

Munich was not altogether without small difficulties of a personal kind. Miss Edgely did not accompany Miss Thorne and Gwendaline on the little excursion up the Zugspitze but remained in her room at the hotel, saying she had letters to write.

"But Edge! It's Germany's highest mountain," Miss Thorne reminds her the evening before when they have a few minutes alone together, Gwenda having gone to wash her hair.

The two ladies have to whisper as the walls are very thin.

"What about the Wine Gardens at Grinzing," Miss Edgely hisses, "how can we go there, you know we always go to Grinzing."

"Keep your voice down Edge deah." Miss Thorne is busy with her travelling flask. "Will you have a teeny one Edge?" she hovers with the tooth glass and the bottle, "I think there is another glass."

"Thanks, I've found it," Miss Edgely snaps, "I'll just have my brandy as usual, thanks all the same."

"Oh Edge! You've been in a frightful huff ever since we left school." Miss Thorne pours a liberal dose for herself. "The gel is very well behaved, you can hardly look on her as a nuisance. I mean, she's so quiet."

"Well, Ella, we usually share a room in Vienna," Miss Edgely pours generously for herself, "and you know perfectly well we can't take her to Grinzing." There are tears in her voice.

"Everything will work well," Miss Thorne says in a low voice, "we're meeting Snow in Vienna, remember? We'll do all the usual things Edge, you'll see."

They drink quickly and in silence.

"Oh! There you are Gwenda. All towelled up!" Miss Thorne answers the polite knock at the door. "All towelled up for the night! Hot milk for you? No? I'll just have a couple of snorts of soda water," Miss Thorne drowns her whisky, "and you Miss Edgely? The same?"

"Thanks! I'm sure!"

"We'll photograph the famous Glockenspiel tomorrow Gwenda," Miss Thorne turns all her attention to the schoolgirl, "it's a beautiful old clock on the Rathaus, the City Town Hall, deah. We must be there early to get into a good picture taking position from across the street. The clock plays a tune, Gwenda, and little painted figures come out on a little platform and dance. You remember the lovely musical clock don't you Miss Edgely?"

"If everyone has finished in the bathroom ... " Miss Edgely takes her towel and her sponge bag and her brandy leaving Miss Thorne chattering to Gwenda and drinking her now lifeless Scotch.

During the long train journey Miss Thorne creates a saint for her school. Perhaps it is the fir trees on the mountain slopes, or the flocks of goats, or the shining onion spire on a pretty church, or some white clouds settling over a distant peak, Miss Thorne is not sure, out of all the passing beauty, what exactly inspires the creation of the saint.

For a moment she remembers the one majestic pine, taller

and straighter and greater than the others back at school. After the first rains the school pines drip and sigh and their fragrance changes. The wet pines are not like the brittle pines unobtrusively shedding long dry needles at the end of the long hot dry summer. Even in their difference they are attractive. Saint Pine, Miss Thorne smiles to herself. That will do very well. Pine Heights will have a saint. The saint's day will be best just before or just after Easter thus making the holiday break one day longer. Not much happens in the autumn term except the epidemics.

She smiles once more. Saint Pine will be a saint to please every one. Saint Pine's Day. Lovely. Her thoughts come quickly, she will order specially woven and embroidered Saint Pine badges for the school hats, and a Saint Pine shield for the Hall, and a stained glass window for the Chapel. A competition, Miss Thorne feels excited, a competition for song writers, the girls can all write songs for Saint Pine and Mr Minsk can set the best ones to music. The song can be sung round Saint Pine.

In her mind, Miss Thorne sees the whole school walking carefully down through the pines to make a circle of reverence round the chosen tree.

There will be colours for the saint. Colours, badges, a flag and a song.

The rhythm of the railway train has a soothing effect. Miss Thorne, trying to concentrate on the changing scenery, slips, in spite of herself, into worrying thoughts about the school. One of the things she must see to is the staffing problem. It is no use to try to discuss it with Miss Edgely. All Edgely can do is to type, with curious mistakes in them, the letters of dismissal, and these have to be dictated. Miss Thorne is unable to decide which of the junior mistresses shall be turned out. It is a question of friendships and money. There are three junior mistresses, all friends, and all bright young women, one even dresses like Electra, all divorced, bringing into the school eight pre-school children between them.

Eight noisy, hungry, little children in the dining room, in the dormitory and in the kindergarten without fees. It is true their mothers' salaries are adjusted but this does not compensate. The cold fact remains that, because of them, eight fee paying children are barred from the overcrowded kindergarten.

"Fees are fees," Miss Thorne murmurs to the pleasing rhythm. At the risk of Edgely's displeasure, because there will be more work for Edge and herself, temporarily, till one mistress (junior), can be found, preferably without offspring, all three, Ms White, Ms Crane and Ms Fortune, Electra, must receive notice to leave. Immediately.

The train, lurching, begins another climb. Miss Thorne does not want to think of the unharmonious. She smiles at the view and at the pale solid girl opposite.

Miss Edgely has given herself up completely to the rhythm. She is lost in some obscurely placed ecstasy.

Miss Thorne closes her eyes. The trouble about being on holiday, living out of suitcases is that one is never sure, unless very methodical, which underclothes have been used. She freshens herself, a dab here and there with her Eau de Cologne.

The week in Munich coincided as planned with part of the Wagner Festival. Thinking of Wagner and of music, Miss Thorne regrets the imminent sacking of Ms Fortune. Soon after she arrived Miss Thorne noticed how pretty she was, especially when flushed and busy on the bath and bedtime evening duty.

The younger children, after their baths, have the privilege of drinking their evening milk in Miss Thorne's large pink-rosed room. They sit on the floor and play with Miss Thorne's own building blocks and some good quality wooden jig saw puzzles. Children of staff are excluded from this happiness.

"Do you know this music?" Miss Thorne asks Ms Fortune as a fresh child is tossed, in her nightdress, through the half

52

open door. Ms Fortune listens, head on one side, half inside the room,

"Yes yes," she says, "it's very nice, I love it. Surely it's the *Siegfried Idyll*, Wagner isn't it?" She is shy and in a hurry. Miss Thorne, who is lying on her big double bed with her heavy tumbler of whisky, pats the eiderdown,

"Lie down and listen," she says, "music is best heard lying down," she invites, "you like Wagner?"

"Oh! I've half a dozen girls in the other bathroom," Ms Fortune disappears.

During the term Miss Thorne prepares a little paper on the *Siegfried Idyll* and delivers it, with Mr Minsk, to the whole school, Mr Minsk playing phrases on the piano when Miss Thorne nods her head in his direction.

This gentle music she tells them was written by Richard Wagner especially for his wife Cosima. It was, she says, known as "The Stairway Music" because a small orchestra, conducted by Wagner himself, performed it on the stairs leading to Cosima's bedroom. The occasion was her birthday and the music was to celebrate the birth of their son one year earlier.

Mr Minsk plays a few bars of the lullaby theme. Miss Thorne continues, explaining that it was composed in great secrecy and rehearsed at a nearby inn.

Mr Minsk obediently plays a little more.

Gwendaline, Miss Thorne reflects, was prepared for the *Siegfried Idyll* but not for *Die Walküre*, not at all. Miss Thorne has of course not questioned her about the music. On purpose she has not discussed it. Perhaps the gel has odd private pictures in her mind about *Die Walküre*. The full rich voices in the electrifying "Ride of the Valkyries" at the opening of the third act do perhaps suggest to the unmusical that they, the Valkyries, are wearing big warm fleecy lined knickers for their aerial flight.

Miss Thorne wonders what Edgely made of the opera. Edge, silly creature, is, as she would put it, "not speaking".

All that has been mentioned so far is that it was first performed at the Munich Opera on 25 June 1870, over a hundred years ago. Miss Thorne explained too that Wagner wrote his own books for his operas. She briefly told the story to Gwendaline, stressing the love music of Siegmund and Siegelinde in Act One, the importance of the music of the storm in the forest, the poignant Wotan's Farewell and the Magic Fire Scene when the circle of fire slowly envelops the sleeping Brünnhilde, bringing the music drama to its close.

The remembered rhythm and the regular sustained beat of the disco mingle with the ever present rhythm of the railway train gathering speed. *All's well now, sweeting; come away to bed.* The thin girl, the one with the long fringe over her eyes, is dancing coming nearer and nearer still ... It's disco, Miss Thorne, it's disco, it's easy Huh! Huh! Huh!

I don't know where you come from
Heaven must have sent you
You held my hand/ You held my hand
When you needed me/ needed me/ needed me . . .

Miss Thorne wakes suddenly at the sound of her own voice croaking.

The engines of the train seem to be pulling back from their own force and holding back the rushing of the train behind them; there is a different sound from the wheels and a different sensation of travel. Miss Thorne has been dreaming, something very intimate, not frightening really, though almost, in its intensity, almost satisfying but not quite, almost on the point of an exquisite feeling. It was only a dream. Which gel? Not one she could think of thank goodness. She wonders if her lunch, perhaps the Wiener Schnitzel in anticipation of Vienna, has been too heavy. Gwenda, opposite, solid in her white dress, is looking out of the window. Miss Edgely is missing, no doubt she is in the lavatory. She usually is there when, after several hours of travelling, the train pulls into a station. A little frown visits Miss Thorne's otherwise untroubled brow when she thinks of the unnecessary delay.

Edgely should not do this always when it is time to be getting their things together. As usual the pleasure of gliding, still with the feeling of immense power but now held in check, alongside the thronged platform into the very heart of an exciting foreign station, will be lost because Edgely will panic and not find her way back to the compartment.

Miss Thorne hopes she did not show outwardly anything of her dream. She tries to remember the Lord's Prayer but it is not the right place for it and she cannot get farther than Thy Kingdom Come.

The Pension Eppelseimer, under the shadow of the Stepansdom, is quietly in readiness for the travellers. Miss Thorne has altered her usual reservation and, for the first two days, has asked for one double room without bath for Miss Snowdon and Miss Edgely, and for two single rooms also without bath for herself and Gwenda. Without bath is an economy.

"We don't travel so far simply to take showers or baths. Oh! everything smells of lilac!" She snorts and sniffs her pleasure and stoutly mounts the stairs to the rooms explaining to Miss Edgely that, in a few days, they will move into the spacious room with three beds, the one they usually have.

The two elderly ladies Lotte and Liselotte Eppelseimer, who keep the establishment, lead the way, bowing and smiling, turning back several times to show their pleasure at seeing Miss Thorne again. All are carrying separate pieces of luggage.

The floor boards are polished and the late afternoon sun lights up the porcelain panels and the hand painted cherubs in the entrance hall. All the rooms look down into a tiny enclosed garden where there are arbours covered in white and purple lilac. "To get into the garden," Miss Thorne explains to Gwenda, "you simply walk downstairs and there is a stone flagged passage which passes by the shop and office on the ground floor. A door at the end of this passage leads directly into the charming and secluded garden. You will love it! May is the best time for this part of the world." Miss Thorne, within sight of the profusion of tossing lilac flowers, feels light and full of youthful enthusiasm.

Miss Snowdon, who has arrived a day before, is waiting at the dinner table.

"How was Munich?" she asks.

"Splendid deah. How was Basle?"

"Lucerne, Prickles!"

"Oh rather! Lucerne of course. Sorry! How silly of me! Gwenda deah, this is Miss Snowdon, Snow deah this is Gwendaline Manners from Pine Heights. Oh! What a journey! And how did "The Placenta"? Well received I hope? Good discussion?"

"Edgely's not coming in to dinner," Miss Snowdon says, "I've arranged for her to have something on a tray."

"That's a good idea, Snow, she's pretty tired." Miss Thorne, with both fists on the lace tablecloth, European fashion, waits for her evening soup which she takes from the tip of the continental soup spoon.

"Soup spoons heah, deah, are not round," quietly she explains to Gwenda, "and we do not put our hand in our laps while eating."

With the coffee and some undefined little sweets wrapped in yellow cellophane, Miss Thorne tells Miss Snowdon about the saint. They are alone together. Gwenda having said "good night", politely, has gone to bed.

"But it takes at least four hundred years for the evolution, or whatever it's called, for a saint."

"How d'you mean?"

"Well, I mean saints don't just come over night."

"Mine," Miss Thorne unwraps a second sweet, "Mine occurred in about two minutes during a tunnel."

While sitting with Miss Snowdon a little longer and smoking one of her black cigars, Miss Thorne confides that she has not had it in her to send the little Manners gel back to school.

"I mean, I haven't told the little gel yet that this is the end of her holiday."

"She's hardly a little gel Prickles," Snowdon, with difficulty, unfastens the hooks on her skirt. "Ah! that's better! I must get on to a diet again. She's hardly little. She's very well developed for her age."

"She's sixteen."

"Oh well, what d'you expect? She'll be wanting boy friends and dancing and Lord knows what."

"No, the trouble is, she doesn't seem to want that sort of thing."

"No?"

"And, what I mean is, I can't really send her orf out on her own while we do the rounds, Grinzing and all that."

"I do see the point. Well, pack her orf back to school then."

"That's not so easy either."

"Well best sleep on it Prickles. Tomorrow is also a day as they say here in Vienna."

I have no pain, Miss Thorne tells herself. The bed is clean and soft and yet she is unable to sleep. She lies quite comfortably and suddenly knows that she is not asleep and will not be able to sleep. Possibly it is the long journey and the oppressive atmosphere accompanied by the rumbling of thunder. She has no headache as Miss Edgely has and as Miss Snowdon, before going to bed, admits to having. Possibly it is the sleeping arrangements; instead of the spacious room with three lilac blessed windows, three beds and comfortable substantial furniture, Miss Thorne feels as if her little room is like an airless cupboard. They are used to being together on holidays and often conduct long and profound conversations on the edge of sleep, conversations which affect all three deeply but are entirely forgotten in the morning.

Miss Thorne knows that, through Gwenda, she has upset everyone.

"It's just a temporary arrangement," Miss Thorne bestowing aspirin and a glass of water, promises Miss Edgely, "when Gwendaline is gone we are to have our usual room."

The thunder rumbles. Summer, in Europe, is the time for thunder storms. The clocks of the city chime during the night and Miss Thorne's little travelling clock ticks away the minutes in a hysteria of time passing. Without wanting them to, thoughts of school come into her mind. The three friends, the three junior mistresses, White, Crane and Fortune, Jannice, Penny and the one who dresses like Electra, all of them so eager, and in their individual ways, good little mothers. And all their children too, all those sturdy little boy children bursting to grow up, unknowing, into the harsh world. In any case, Miss Thorne reflects, she only takes little boys in the kindergarten as Pine Heights is a school for girls. The little boys could not stay for long for this reason. She thinks too about the three young women, how, not so very long ago all of them must have been pleased, excited, delighted to be loved and chosen and to be married. And all three have, more than once, for love and other mysterious reasons, gone through the bearing of their children. In the first place the months of carrying the child and then the giving birth to the child, and, even more arduous perhaps, the task of caring and feeding and other additional burdens attached in general to the bringing up of children. It is not the first time that Miss Thorne has been confronted by this apparent paradox of human behaviour. And here she was stout and well fed, able to travel twice a year as a rule, as cheaply as possible of course but comfortably; here she was lying in bed contemplating the terminating of their employment. Perhaps ending, if only temporarily, their livelihood.

Miss Thorne, not liking to do it, always sacks people

quickly. She tells them they can leave the next day or on the same night if preferred as there is an awkwardness, she feels, in sitting at meals with people you have sacked.

She reasons with herself turning her large well-cared-for body over in the narrow bed; that is part of the trouble this narrow bed. She is accustomed to a double bed to herself. She reasons that her school will not be able to continue to make ends meet. One mistress can do what these three are doing at present and, for a time, all must be dispensed with. She will teach the French and the self expression dancing herself and do the bedtime duty. Edge should be able, though it is doubtful, to do turns of evening duties. And though she is unable to teach she could supervise silent reading and study periods and piano practice.

As the night progresses Miss Thorne feels less able about the dancing and the French, beginners and advanced, as well as the maths, Latin and literature she is doing in addition to all the administrative duties. There is too the standard of the quality of Pine Heights. The girl, Debbie Frome, is not exactly suitable material for Pine Heights; Miss Thorne knows that she must cultivate the material; consideration must be given to the cheques from Mr Frome. This is even more important in the light of the fact that Mr Manners' recently written one was not honoured by the bank.

Turning over in the little bed again Miss Thorne is completely honest with herself as she considers her problems and knows where she is not being entirely straight forward. Miss Edgely should go really. Even if discouraged brutally Miss Edgely would never leave. For one thing she has simply nowhere in the world where she can go. Facing this, Miss Thorne knows that, without Edgely, she herself has no one. There is Miss Snowdon, but Miss Snowdon, living and working in a different situation, could suddenly surprise everyone and marry, a wealthy surgeon perhaps. Such things were not unknown.

The thunder comes closer and lightning flashes light up

the small room. It is impossible to sleep; the room is simply a cupboard.

The thunder crashes; it is overhead and seems to split the house. Nothing has split, Miss Thorne's bedroom door is open, that is all. Someone has opened it. In the next flash of lightning Miss Thorne sees Gwendaline in her white night-dress standing just inside the doorway. She is sobbing.

Miss Thorne sits up, the bed creaks violently as if it will give way.

"Why Gwenda! What is the matter deah?"

Gwendaline closes the door and rushes over to the bedside and, falling on her knees, flings both arms over the white counterpane. In the next lightning flash her hair shines as if with a light of its own. Thunder rolls. Miss Thorne pats the girl's shoulder,

"It's all right Gwenda, it's only a storm."

"I know, I'm scared. I'm silly to be so frightened."

"Come along, I'll take you back to your own bed," Miss Thorne throws off her covers and gets up from her bed.

"Please, oh Please let me stay with you."

"You will be perfectly all right, Gwenda, in your own bed."

Miss Thorne gently guides the frightened girl back to her own little room. Ennobling thoughts and feelings rise in her breast as she realizes that she can explain to Gwenda that fear is a perfectly natural feeling but there is absolutely no need to be frightened of anything, especially not of thunder.

In Gwendaline's room there is another terrific crash and, after it, a downpour of rain; the heavy pattering of the rain on the leaves and on the roofs of the arbours is a relief. From outside, through the partly open window, there is the smell of the rain. The scent from the soaked lilac is intoxicating.

Miss Thorne, with an arm round the shoulders of the trembling girl, leads her towards the rumpled bed. Sitting down into the middle of the bed, she opens her arms to the girl, embracing her and drawing her close.

"Tell me about Wagner," Miss Thorne says to Gwenda, "Tell me how you feel about Wagner and his music. Did you like his music? Did you Gwenda?"

Music would be appropriate, Miss Thorne, taking up most of the mattress, is thinking. The dawn is filled with birds even though they are in the city of Vienna. Well there is music, she thinks, after all, birds are singing in the lilac trees and in a nearby park; their song transcends the sounds of the big city as it comes to life after the night. Even if it is not the *Siegfried Idyll* it is a sweet sweet music, this bird song.

The night was idyllic, tender, hilarious and ludicrous. There was the laughing and the trying not to laugh; it would not have done to disturb everyone in the Pension.

After the storm the night was tranquil. Then suddenly the bed gave way, not the whole bed, but simply, with a slight but prolonged jangling, all the springs fell, littering the oiled boards of the floor. Miss Thorne and Gwenda, their bodies sagging together through the widening space, were resting on the floor.

"Better go to my room," Miss Thorne managed to gasp. She had laughed till her face was wet with tears. Gwenda, surprisingly, had more sense. It is better to break only one bed, hers. Why not finish the night on the mattress on the floor.

"There would be more room to turn over if we want to."

"Yes you are quite right, deah."

Laughing and apologizing for the heavy, well-fed school girl, Miss Thorne explains about the bed at the breakfast table.

"*Sie ist,* how you say, *eine Valkyrie,*" the older woman, the mother, who keeps the Pension, unashamedly, in front of them all, caresses, with the back of her freckled hand, the full curve of Gwenda's breast. Miss Thorne, a little proud and more than a little fond, looks on with approval. There is an attractive blush spreading on Gwenda's smooth white neck.

No, No, Gwenda assures them, she is not hurt at all. Not a bit hurt, only worried because the bed is broken.

The old woman, continuing to smooth Gwenda's full white blouse, is distressed at the inconvenience to her guests. She tells Miss Thorne in slow careful German, smiling at them all in turn, that tonight their usual large room will be ready for them and that the young *Fraülein Valkyrie* is to have the other small room where the bed is stronger. The sight of the old woman's hand lingering on Gwenda and Gwenda's little pink flush spreading disturbs Miss Thorne, though she does not show this outwardly at all. She breaks her crisp white breakfast roll and spreads it generously with butter. Even more disturbing is the regret she feels that they are able to have their large room sooner than expected.

"Are you feeling better today Edge deah?" she asks, passing Miss Edgely the tea she insists on having. "Yes please I will have the honey, thank you Gwenda."

As she drinks her coffee she thinks to herself, with her usual honesty, that she must get Gwenda back to Pine Heights without delay and that she must, afterwards, use the time in Vienna wisely. The complications are twofold about Gwenda remaining at school; one is the development of the personal involvement which, if it deepens and there is every possibility that it might, will be painful to break and the other is simply money if Mr Manners, for some reason, finds himself in the position of being unable to supply it.

And then, of course, there is Edgely.

With her second cup of coffee Miss Thorne realizes she must immerse herself in the different museums, the enormous Kunsthistoriches Museum, for example, she has never spent enough time there. Then there is the Beethoven museum and the Haydn museum and the Museum des 20

Jahrhunderts where she has never been because the meaning of modern art has always eluded her. She resolves to bring herself up to date with the contemporary painters and sculptors. She will walk daily and walk and walk in the gardens of the Schönbrunn.

"Simply I must pull myself together," Miss Thorne tells herself.

Gwenda is packing her things to move across to the tiny room opposite which has been quickly cleaned and prepared for her with fresh towels and bed linen. Miss Thorne appears at the open door. The broken bed has been cleared away.

"May I come in Gwenda?"

"Of course Miss Thorne," the girl kneeling on the floor beside her open suitcase looks suddenly very young. She looks small and vulnerable as she smiles up at Miss Thorne.

Miss Thorne closes the door and leans against it. She hardly feels able to say what she has to say.

"Gwenda," she says, "Gwenda, you will have two days here in Vienna to see and to learn something of the city and the culture and then I shall have to pack you orf to Pine Heights."

"But . . . "

"No buts please, Gwenda." Looking down at the girl, Miss Thorne thinks how she would like to be able to provide for her, immediately, all that the girl wants. Just the simple innocent wish, the secret and shy wish spoken of during the night, which of course might not come. She thinks of the lines from Goethe:

And she on the torrent's edge in childish simplicity,
In a little hut in a little alpine field
And all her household things
Gathered in that small world.

These lines came to her almost with pain during the night when Gwenda confided that what she wished for most in the world was a kind husband and four babies. Miss Thorne is

63

amazed to discover that such a simple and unsophisticated wish exists in anyone's heart.

"I have various things to do here Gwenda, study things and so on. I am arranging for you to fly back . . . "

"Oh!" the girl cries out, "Is it because of last night?"

"No Gwenda, not because of that, though that must never happen again, you understand. It was the storm, it was the storm, d'you see."

"It wasn't only the storm," the girl springs to her feet. "It wasn't only the storm. You were pleased, you said so, you told me things, you talked to me like you were happy with me . . . "

"It was the storm Gwenda," Miss Thorne is severe but her lips tremble. "Remember the storm Gwenda and that I told you never to be afraid of anything."

Tears fill Gwenda's eyes and overflow from her fair, almost white eye lashes. Miss Thorne, trembling, looks away.

"I don't want to go back all on my own without you. Miss Thorne I don't want to go. I want to stay with you, please. I'm very quiet, aren't I. Please let me stay," her voice is flat and low and, as she speaks, she begins to cry, still in the same low voice, busily folding her clothes and yet not managing to do anything with them. "I've never been happy before like I have been on this holiday. I've never had a friend before, I mean a real friend. I thought you were my friend, I thought you really liked me. I thought last night you were happy like I was. I like going places with you, Miss Thorne, I feel safe when you smile at me even when other people are there, like you smile at me through those people. Like in the train yesterday, like last night. Please Miss Thorne don't send me away, don't send me back all alone."

"But Gwenda, my deah gel, we, Miss Edgely and Miss Snowdon and I have arranged to do a lot of study, dull things, after you have gorn, cemeteries and things like that . . . "

"I don't mind, Miss Thorne, I really like cemeteries and grave stones. Please let me stay with you. I'll keep out of your way when you and Miss Edgely and Miss Snowdon want to be on your own. I'll stay by the grave stones. I'll sit in the cemetery. Don't say awful things like 'after you've gone,' I won't go. I won't!"

Have you travelled? the novelist wanted to know. In among the people on the rush-hour platform Miss Peabody tried to turn her mind from the suburban trains as they made the repetitive journeys up to London and back down through all the stations away from London. She tried to think of the excitement and the dignity of foreign travel as Diana Hopewell would know it. She found it more comforting to think of the novelist somewhere out on her land. The lonely horseback rider. Perhaps the horse was cream coloured with a short black mane and a black tail to match. Something smart in horses, cream and black or black with light tan; something smart in horses as in the fashion houses in Oxford Street.

Foreign travel, foreign languages, foreign food the idea of it all fascinated Miss Peabody; it worried her too. It was more comfortable to let her mind return to, and to roam on, the slopes of the novelist's shallow valley, hearing only the crows and the occasional soft conversation of the doves.

Our magpie, the novelist wrote, has a lovely liquid song like softly running water. A little, I should think, like your curlew. Miss Peabody had never heard or seen a curlew.

"Curlews?" Mr Bains said in the office. Sometimes he drank his morning coffee there with one eyebrow raised in the direction of Miss Truscott. Miss Peabody, dying to talk about the novelist, restrained herself and asked brightly, had anyone heard the curlew lately?

"Currrlews?" Mr Bains repeated the word. "Och! Scotland The Brave!" he turned on his Scottish acent.

" 'The rank is but the guinea stamp. A marn's a marn for a' that . . . ' Rabbie Burrrns, Scotland the Brave! 'The rarnk is but . . . ' "

"Bains," Mr Barrington's voice called softly from the inner office and Mr Bains slipped through the door.

The crows, Miss Peabody thought mainly about them, crows in the distance and crows coming closer.

One day, the novelist wrote, you must travel. There is a little mountain, she wrote, the Kahlenberg, near Vienna, I'll explain about it. It is quite easy to go there by motor coach or there are buses. From the Kahlenberg there is the most complete and panoramic view of Vienna. In the twilight, at dusk, it is heavenly; there lies the whole of Vienna at your feet. The river Danube is like a misty blue path round the city and all round are the famous Vienna woods, the Wiener Wald.

"You don't really want to send me away," Gwenda tells Miss Thorne, "you are really happy with me, I can tell when you're happy," she says in a purring voice beside her Head-mistress.

They are all delighted with the view from the Kahlenberg. It is a fine warm night, fresh after the thunderstorm the night before. Stars, as if for the tourists, begin to litter the sky. The air excites Miss Thorne.

"You know, you are suffering from what we at Pine Heights call A Crush," she says, almost in a whisper, to the girl.

"Am I?" Gwenda, very close to Miss Thorne, squats almost on Miss Thorne's feet. She looks up at her smiling.

Miss Edgely and Miss Snowdon are both feeling better.

"Keep still," Miss Edgely says to Miss Thorne, "and I'll snap you like that."

"Hold it!" says Miss Snowdon and she takes a picture of Edgely taking one of Thorne.

Gwenda's smile reminds Miss Thorne of the eager little smile, and what she understood about it, several years ago. Gwenda was ill in bed during an epidemic.

"I give 'em bowl of soup each," the gardener said to Miss Thorne who instinctively wanted to correct him: I gave them all bowls of soup, Bales, there are not two gels in the Sanatorium with German measles but twelve. She corrected him in her head. Aloud she said,

"Thank you Bales," and meant it because he had, at short notice, combined his outside work with the duties of the then Matron who had left the night before. Thinking about it Miss Thorne is unable to remember why that Matron was sacked, some foolish indiscretion, no doubt.

It is Gwenda's smile she is remembering; remembering too how the child suddenly stopped smiling when she realized, without her spectacles, that the person looking round the half open door of the sick room was not her mother, as she had thought, in her short sightedness, but simply her Headmistress doing the rounds of the school sanatorium. Miss Thorne, at the time, understanding immediately the mistake in the eager smile and its sudden ending, tried to be something a little more than merely a hardly known Headmistress. The little girl, recently motherless, was not used to not having a mother and often forgot the fact. Miss Thorne understood the pain of the equally sudden remembering. She tucked Gwenda's doll into the bed beside her, asked what name the doll had, and then gave its wooden face an absurd little kiss which amused Gwenda. Miss Thorne, in her way of seeing everything, noticed the little girl trying to show that she was pleased and amused. After all, it was not usual for a Headmistress to play.

This incident has served Miss Thorne well through the years; it is the kind of memory she is able to summon at will to give her strength and direction at times.

Bales, she reflects all these years later, as well as being ungrammatical, was lying disgracefully. He could not have given out bowls of soup, there was not a drop of soup in the place, the invalid diet at the time of the German measles being bread and margarine and weak tea.

But why, on the Kahlenberg, on such a heavenly night, so filled with delicious feelings and fragance, fill one's mind with Bales. It is the smile she is thinking of, and the repetition of the smile. She returns the smile now with one of her kindest.

The Kahlenberg restores friendship and harmony; the evening soup is taken pleasantly.

But, the novelist pointed out to Miss Peabody, Edgely thinks Gwenda is being sent back to school and Gwenda has been smiled at by Miss Thorne in such a way that she feels sure she is going to be allowed to stay and finish the tour.

She ventures the remark, while the soup plates are being removed, that London must be simply super.

"It is," Miss Snowdon replies. She is wondering what the latest development is.

Miss Peabody sniffed eagerly at the pages of the novelist's letter, longing for the now familiar fragrance. Perhaps it was something Diana was drinking, a golden liquid in a tiny glass, which scented the letters.

I am afraid that this is a very crowded canvas, the novelist started a fresh sheet of paper, that is a frightful cliché but a true one, she wrote. The thing about clichés is that often there is not a better way of expressing oneself. I am sure you will agree. Though, as a writer, I should avoid them.

Miss Peabody whose life, not from her own fault at all, had become a series of clichés and platitudes, agreed. It takes all sorts to make the world go round, she started her own reply on her blue writing paper.

"Dotty! Dotty!" her mother's voice pierced the tranquility. "Dotty! You never washed the potato saucepan tonight. I never heard you washing up the potato saucepan!"

"Coming mother," Dorothy Peabody quietly put her pen down. It was true, skimping the dishes to get everything out of the way quickly, she had pushed the old black pan under the sink.

It was some time before she was able to be peacefully back in her bedroom with the new letter and her preparations for a reply.

Writers don't have any friends, the novelist wrote, and any friends the writer has don't read what that writer has written.

Oh! Miss Peabody gasped at the pain of this. She took up her pen. Oh Diana, she wrote, I am your Friend and I read every word you write many many times. I love your writing . . . she put down her pen.

The novelist's handwriting sprawled over several pages. Miss Peabody began to reread the letter,

All three of them, Snowdon, Thorne and Edgely, the novelist continued, have reached that age when people give each other expensive pots of unusual jam or packets of cress seed to sow on sponges as presents. They have different ways of shopping too. Miss Thorne, when she shops, say in Venice, has something expensive in coloured venetian glass packed and shipped back to Pine Heights. She is accustomed to making purchases on behalf of other people. For example, before leaving for the holiday she has six pairs of white pantyhose put on Gwendaline Manners' bill, "so that the gel has plenty of changes", she tells Edgely. There is always the possibility that the bill will be paid, if not by Mr Manners, by someone else. It is wise, Miss Thorne makes the point to Miss Edgely, to keep bills supplied with items up to date. In the event of payment being forthcoming, an account with nothing on it is useless.

White stockings are worn at Pine Heights. Miss Thorne

has special ones, pantyhose, made for herself and for two very large girls who are, under her wing, on a lemon, oatmeal and hot water diet.

Edgely, when she is shopping, does it privately. She searches miserably for meaningless gifts in department stores which are the same in every country. She buys things as presents which everyone can buy anywhere. Furthermore, though she would never tell Ella Thorne, instead of original paintings or prints she buys cheap replicas or posters of paintings. She enjoys a few moments of secret happiness because she has not spent as much as Miss Thorne.

I am not sure about Snowdon, the novelist wrote, she is a bit of a closed book to me at present. There I go again with the old cliché. Snowdon's paper, by the way, "The Forgotten Placenta" or whatever it was, inspired Miss Thorne to prepare a small offering, for the sixth form girls only, to be given together with an abstract from Miss Snowdon's. Miss Thorne has written a lecture called "Chasing The Orgasm: How When And Where". She has the idea of an evening, next term, with the two lectures, if Miss Snowdon is willing, being a hospital matron makes her so suitable, and, as she puts it, some perfectly frank discussion.

I shall have to be careful, the novelist added in small writing to squeeze as much as possible on to the bottom of the last page, about the clichés; in future I shall underline them with a red pen. Also I have to admit that I shall probably not manage this time to hit the peak in pornography as in the love in the saddle scenes in *Angels etc*.

Miss Peabody was too shocked by certain words to read on for a while. Diana had indeed underlined some phrases in red ink and the result was dazzling. Miss Peabody could not write either, though she was longing to start her reply. The evening, belonging to the novelist, was hers too. Her mother's snores came across the landing with a splendid regularity. She sighed. It had not been a good day. Perhaps she should try and write it down,

Sometimes I have lunch with Miss Truscott, she wrote. I was meant to have lunch with her today. We don't go anywhere elaborate, just round the corner you know, somewhere quick, just the two of us. I feel it's a bit of an honour really if she singles me out. But twice running now, at the last minute, she has let me down and gone with Mr Bains. He called for her today and she said, "Coming Mr Bains. Be there in half a sec," and off she went to do things to herself in the Ladies, the Worth perfume, all that, forgetting all about our little arrangement. The office did seem dreary, I can tell you, so I thought I would keep my pecker up and go out in the lunch hour and do a bit of shopping. It's so easy to be lost in the big stores and I get so het up not knowing what to get. Mother can't eat anything if it has starch, nuts or ginger in it. She cries if I give her flowers, says they are slowly dying in the vase, says it breaks her heart to see them. "Dotty don't give me flowers," she always says; once she cried for a week about some carnations.

Miss Truscott's birthday and Mrs Brewer's are in the same month as mother's. It's always the same at this time of the year, off my head not knowing what to get. And then there's Christmas . . . Miss Truscott's present . . .

How could the embarrassment of giving something too expensive, out of all proportion, to Miss Truscott, be avoided. It would be unbearable to give something shoddy or cheap. Miss Truscott had once left a present, not Miss Peabody's, thank goodness, behind in the office. It was clear it was too awful a gift for her to take home. What sort of thing could be given, a tea service or a tin opener.

Miss Peabody to her surprise, some hours later, found she had written quite a long letter to the novelist. Afraid to relive the agony she did not read it through and so was not aware, having a terribly short memory, of exactly what her letter contained.

The novelist's reply, therefore, about ten days later, gave her a surprise. The letter was short but crashed black all over the paper.

Am in a tearing hurry, the writing hardly stayed on the page, it's the approach to drama in the Thorne, Manners, Edgely affair, but felt I must set your mind at rest re those worrying presents. Have sent off, Air Freight, two dozen jars of honey from my bees. Sometimes my valley positively drips with honey. You can smell it everywhere. You'll see there are different varieties; Red Gum, White Gum, Blackbutt, Rape Seed, Cape Weed and Clover. Rape seed, like its name, is particularly good. And there are three sheep-skins. I've had them dyed black, red and purple, good little bed-side rugs. No worries now about the gifts. Hey? Honey very good for an invalid ma? Do you good too. I'll send over a couple more sheepskins, plain. You can have a jacket and boots made; set you up for the winter, see how the office likes them!

Now Back To The Drawing Board Back to Vienna and my Troubles. *Auf Wiedersehen*!

Miss Peabody sat up at the dressing table. The summer night was chilly but in her heart was a warmth. Such a warmth she had never experienced in her life before. She could not believe that anyone could be so generous and take so much trouble for her, Dorothy Peabody. Her pale timid eyes shone back at her from the tarnished mirror.

During the week Miss Peabody had borrowed a book from the public library. She read again the passage she wanted:

Artemis. Diana. Folk Goddess of the Grecians. Daughter of Zeus. She copied it out on to her blue writing pad in her round, even handwriting; the handwriting the novelist had said she was in love with.

"My handwriting is nice, though I do say it myself," Miss Peabody murmured, rearranging the beautiful words:

Artemis. Diana. Folk Goddess of the Grecians. Daughter of Zeus.

Artemis, Diana,
Folk Goddess of the Grecians
Daughter of Zeus.
— Diana. —

The Lord of Free Nature. She goes hunting on the mountains with her group of nymphs. She lives with them in the grove and in the paddock. She is related to the cultivation of trees and is the Goddess of Fertility.

She also appears later as the Goddess of Birth. She appears in Sculpture as an armoured young woman; a Huntress with a short pleated skirt and a bow and arrow and is surrounded by animals. She is both the Goddess of Virgins and the Goddess of Birth.

She is the sister of Apollo.

She is also Goddess of the Moon.

All this was Diana. Miss Peabody was amazed and full of admiration.

There seemed to be some contradiction but this did not worry Miss Peabody. Contradictions made the Goddess human.

The contradictions make you even more splendid, she wrote at the end of the account of Diana, and signed her name.

She found that, for the first time in her life, she was looking forward to her mother's birthday, and to Miss Truscott's and to Mrs Brewer's.

"Dotty! Dotty! Dotty! I've been calling and calling," her mother's querulous voice interrupted the dream of Diana.

"Yes mother, I'm coming directly," Miss Peabody plodded down to the kitchen to make the warm milk. She was on her knees a long time by her mother's bed. The old lady wanted to pray but had forgotten what comes after "Thy will be done on Earth as it is in Heaven." She said she knew it was something vital and that she must remember it as she couldn't live without it. She refused to listen to her daughter.

"It's bread mother," Dorothy prompted.

"No dear, no thank you, not just now dear, let me see, Thy will be done on Earth as it is in Heaven."

"Bread mother," Dorothy breathed the word. "Bread."

"No thank you dear, you know I never eat at night, not even a teeny sandwich, not after my milk, why! you know I'd be awake all night."

Patiently Dorothy stayed by her mother till, worn out with trying to remember, she allowed Dorothy to say the prayer.

Like Thorne, the novelist wrote to Miss Peabody, I would not mind at all hanging the Edgelys of this world by their necks like fowls before they are plucked.

Miss Thorne feels that Miss Edgely will hold her back from doing things which are useful and good as well as pleasing. Edgely is becoming an obstacle.

Miss Thorne's motives towards Gwenda are developing along lines which I had not envisaged. Miss Thorne is showing a side to her nature which I did not know existed.

"Tomorrow Gwenda," Miss Thorne pauses on the landing outside Gwenda's little room, "Miss Snowdon, Miss Edgely and I shall be visiting the central cemetery and a few other places deserving our study and devotion to research." She watches Snowdon and Edgely as they move on together down the passage to the large room at the end.

"I shall return in a few moments, if I may, Gwenda, to say good night," she adds graciously.

"Thank you Miss Thorne."

"It's Grinzing tomorrow or isn't it," Miss Edgely says to Miss Thorne when they are all three together in their room.

"Oh rather!" Miss Thorne says after an awkward little silence.

"But what about the gel?" Miss Snowdon asks.

"Yes, you did promise to send her back to school and she's still here." Edgely is indignant; "How can we take her to the Wine Festival! What would they think at school!"

Miss Thorne does not say that she is the one who does the thinking at school.

"Now Edge!" she says, "everything's all right. All right, Edge! Yes we are going to Grinzing tomorrow, let's no more of this!"

"Ah! Shakespeare!" Miss Snowdon is getting undressed.

"Misquoted, I'm afraid," Miss Thorne says.

"May I come in Gwenda?"

"Of course Miss Thorne."

The girl is already in her nightgown, her clothes neatly folded, Pine Heights fashion, over the back of her chair. She smiles at the Headmistress.

"Perhaps you would like to write your letters and postcards tomorrow Gwenda. You could spend the day sitting in one of those charming little arbours in the garden. Just now the lilac is heavenly after the rain."

"Yes, Miss Thorne," Gwenda stands and smiles.

Miss Thorne has not forgotten the holidays at Pine Heights with Gwenda, sometimes three times in a year, in a sensible routine of walks and study, not too much study, a translation or two and some drawing, still life perhaps, enduring the loneliness of the empty school, receiving from time to time picture postcards covered all over with neat, round handwriting bearing incredibly dull news from self-absorbed girls who were travelling, or staying happily, with mothers and fathers, aunts, grandmothers or older sisters. Sterile postcards.

Miss Thorne feels an hour of revenge is near. She would like to join Gwenda in the writing of these postcards. It would be nice, she thinks, to have a new biro and squeeze into the small spaces available meaningless words and uninteresting messages to be received by those who had sent them to Gwenda when she badly needed the companionship of a living letter.

"You will enjoy writing your letters Gwenda," Miss Thorne gives the girl a searching look. "I want you to have a nice day tomorrow, deah."

"Can I stay with you, still?" Gwenda asks. "Please?" Miss Thorne is not sure how to reply.

"I intend to offer you an explanation Gwenda," she says, "I think we should not discuss now, simply speak our 'good night' only. It is time for sleep now."

"Good night Miss Thorne," Gwenda says, stepping forward at the same time as Miss Thorne.

"Good night Gwenda," for a moment Miss Thorne feels the clinging girl in her embrace. Gently she disentangles herself, holding Gwenda by the shoulders at arms' length.

"Good night deah," she says with a little laugh, aware of the shakiness of her own voice.

Miss Thorne makes her way slowly along the passage to the end room. She thinks the best thing would be to write a calm and cheerful letter to the girl. She remembers the touchingly innocent things Gwenda is wishing for in her life, a kind husband, her own house with a garden and four, or was it five, babies. She twists her mouth into a wry little smile. All those years with the intellectual and musical background of Pine Heights . . . and the gel wants simply the kitchen, the ironing board and the baby bath.

All the same, it is the way in which Gwenda confided her wishes which has moved Miss Thorne. She does not want to send Gwenda back to school, but she must because of Edgely. Miss Snowdon too deserves her holiday on the terms they have always agreed upon.

Miss Edgely is sitting on the side of her bed.

"I'm cold," she complains.

"But Edge, it's summer over heah, you can't be cold!" Miss Thorne prepares for bed skillfully.

"I am so! Warm me!"

Miss Thorne who has a half written letter to Gwenda in her head is unwilling. Miss Snowdon's corner of the room is in darkness.

"Oh well," Miss Thorne says, switching off the remaining lights, "Oh well, I'll come in for a few minutes then."

"Not if you don't want to."

"Now Edge, don't be difficult and sulky! Move over a bit, I've said I'll come in."

It takes considerable time to soothe Miss Edgely. When at last she is asleep, Miss Thorne is free to write her letter. Putting on the small lamp by her own bed, she writes,

Dear Gwenda,

No doubt you will find it strange to receive a letter from your Headmistress especially since we are travelling together and seeing each other every day. It is because we are not really seeing each other every day that I am writing to you. I want to explain to you, Gwenda, that the Night of the Thunderstorm was in a sense a night on its own. The night can be treasured but, at the same time it is something to be put away, tucked safely in the memory as something belonging to those things which are not within the power of repetition.

I have known you, Gwenda, for several years and I am very fond of you. I have commitments in all sorts of directions, as you will know, from being at school. I have personal involvements too which do not leave me entirely free. That is my side of it.

Now for your side.

You are very young and you are pretty. Yes pretty, even though you yourself don't think so; you have a sweet smile. When you smile, as you did on the Kahlenberg, your whole face lights up. Remember this and remember to smile often.

You must look forward with happiness to the future. Be patient. A nice true friend, as you told me you wished for, will come along for you. Remember that all people go through lonely times at some time or another.

You must enjoy your day in the garden. I shall try to come back early in order to take you to the famous amusement park, the Prater.

Before you go back to school Gwenda, and quite firmly I do have to despatch you, (I have appointments to keep in Paris and in London) I shall take you to the cemetery here to see the graves of Beethoven and Brahms, Schubert, Johann Strauss, Von Suppé and Hugo Wolf — all these famous musicians are buried close to one another. And, nearby is a memorial to Mozart!

Here I am starting to give you a lecture on these beautiful yet simple grave stones when I really want to write that it has given me pleasure to see you enjoying yourself on our little tour. I want to write too that I am perfectly calm about your going back to school the day after tomorrow. I think it advisable for you to be calm too.

Miss Thorne stops writing her letter. She realizes she is far from calm. She has a strong wish to go from the big room along the passage to the little room. She supposes Gwenda is sweetly asleep and she smiles as she thinks of this.

Reading through her letter, correcting the punctuation, Miss Thorne feels it is a mixture of a cheap fortune teller, a salacious correspondent addressing "Anxious Blue Eyes" or "Deserted" in the back pages of a popular magazine and a paid museum guide. She knows, however, that hidden behind the carefully measured tread of her letter are real feelings and real passion. And, who should know better than an avid scholar of literature exactly what kind of warning was in the thunder storm.

She knows that it will not do to give Gwenda the letter. She must talk to her instead. She slips the pages under the embroidered dressing table cover to hide it for the time being.

*　　*　　*

Miss Thorne has not had much wine and is in danger of being out of favour with Miss Edgely and Miss Snowdon. The crowded wine houses and the tubs of flowers, the sentimental songs and the strolling, laughing, accordion players irritate Miss Thorne. She is trying not to show her irritation. She reasons that it is perfectly natural for Miss Edgely to want her holiday to include things she likes. During the slow hours Miss Thorne finds herself thinking of Gwenda alone at the Pension. It will be a long day even if spent in the garden.

The pleasure of the day for Miss Thorne will be to see Gwenda's pleasure when she experiences, for the first time, the extraordinary Viennese entertainment, the carnival and the Prater. Because Miss Thorne did not give her letter to Gwenda, she, Gwenda, does not know of Miss Thorne's intention. The idea of surprising the girl adds to Miss Thorne's private pleasure and excitement.

As well as caring deeply for Gwenda, Miss Thorne finds herself thinking of Debbie Frome and the way she has of peering through her long fringe. She has not lost, in migration, her north of England accent and direct way of speaking. Even after some weeks at Pine Heights she has not lost the way she has of moving her shoulders. Miss Thorne thinks about the bony shoulders moving, shrugging forward in a provocative manner, first one and then the other, so different from Gwenda's slow-moving, massive body. A reflection on the carbohydrates at Pine Heights? Miss Thorne raises her eyebrows. Possibly.

Gwenda so badly needs some of the Frome girl's self confidence and some of that look of security in the knowledge of the expectation of happiness which brings happiness or which is happiness. There are possibilities ahead for Gwenda if only she can learn to lean forward in the Frome manner and take them.

Miss Thorne sees immense possibilities for her girls at all times, but mostly on Sundays when they enter the school chapel like swans in their white dresses. These dresses seem to stand out and float round the strong, young, solid, girlish bodies.

Immense possibilities. Miss Thorne always stands watching with pleasure and approval as the girls go to their places.

Immensitie cloystered in thy deare womb. She knows the quotation is not quite right for this stage of their development but she likes the words. Poetic references pass through her mind. She changes the quotation to suit present day needs.

"Immensitie cloystered in their hearts," she says to herself in the porch of the chapel, "many of these gels have no intention of devoting themselves to motherhood."

It is typical, significant, that Debbie Frome's dress is not of the same material as the other white frocks. Hers is of some kind of expensive Italian knitted cotton and clings in a revealing, and at the same time, attractive way to her spirited body. The gel, Miss Thorne notices, dances disco rhythm to her pew in chapel.

If only the two gels could become friends. She might then invite them both to accompany her to Europe next May. Together they might even visit the sophisticated night clubs in Vienna where there would be music and dancing to enliven Gwenda. Miss Thorne thinks of the Wagner Festival in Bayreuth. It would be splendid to see the effect Wagner would have on Debbie Frome. Perhaps some time. Miss Thorne smiles.

"Pensive Prickles?" Miss Snowdon is returning with Miss Edgely along the flower laden path from the wine house.

"*Ein Viertel* Dear?" Miss Edgely carries two quarter litre mugs of cold white wine. Miss Snowdon also carries two.

"First one down the hatch has the extra!" she sits on the ornamental bench next to Miss Thorne. Miss Edgely sits on the other side.

"Dawdling, Dreaming and Drinking," Miss Snowdon sighs. "Penny for your thoughts Prickles?"

"Oh! she's ah thinking of ah someone beginning with ah G." Miss Edgely takes her wine, in gulps; "You need more wine dear," Miss Edgely says, "you do know, don't you, it doesn't shoot you not to have enough." She giggles, "There's plenty more where that came from. I mean, that's what a wine festival's all about isn't it. So drink and be merry!"

Miss Thorne looks at Miss Edgely's flushed face and tries not to associate Miss Edgely's once new and unusual experience many years ago, which pleased Miss Thorne very much then, with the present pleasure of caring for Gwenda and the introduction, the initiation, to new experience to which Miss Thorne is looking forward.

"Say gels!" Miss Thorne makes an effort to put her little plan forward. "Say gels!" Miss Edgely and Miss Snowdon are not able to hear. An American girl, surrounded by an admiring group of Viennese young men, is singing,

"Wien! Wien! shtatt ob my dreems. Wien! Wien Leeber Wien! Ole!"

Her accent is appalling, nauseating is the word Miss Thorne uses inside her head.

"Say gels," Miss Thorne tries again, "what say yew we go try the Prater this evo? My shout!" the simulated Australian accent betrays anxiety.

"Good Grief Prickles!" Miss Snowdon is tipping half the extra *Viertel* into Edgely's glass. "We always stay late here Prickles! We always stay till the witching hour!" she says in surprise.

"I am thinking," Miss Thorne says too calmly for the other two, "that I would like to get back to the Pension. I think we should, all of us, go out for a nice meal somewhere and then on to the Prater. Meals too, interesting ones, are part of a holiday. Cream of mushroom soup? or perhaps, *Suppe mit Griessnockerl* and a tender *Wiener Schnitzel*, Miss Thorne warms to her subject, "tiny new potatoes with parsley and butter and a salad plate of those lovely little tomatoes and to finish, you remember, the omelettes served with heaps of jam and sprinkled with sugar, what were they called? *Kaiserschmarren! Kaiserschmarren* and then on to the Prater. It would be an experience for Gwenda to take back to school. An experience I would like her to have."

"Oh Gwenda! Gwendah! Gwendah!" Miss Edgely interrupts.

"Now Edge," Miss Thorne raises her voice. "No Tantrums in the park!" A group of students, passing, laugh with the good nature which is prevalent in the gardens.

"Oh, it's like having to tell Mr Frome that you don't need to learn the language to play French cricket," Miss Thorne turns away. The others, not understanding, follow her as she walks with purpose through the park. Both her way of walking and her travelling costume, an ample jacket and skirt in blue denim (it has an accompanying set of white drip dry blouses) are out of place.

The day at Grinzing has never ended abruptly like this before.

"I said all along it would be a mistake to bring a schoolgirl on the trip. We never have in the past." Miss Edgely tells anyone passing, that is anyone who can understand English. "I said all along it would be a mistake to bring a schoolgirl . . . " Tourists thus accosted are soon running in all directions.

During the long tram ride back Miss Snowdon feels peace should be restored.

"I for one Prickles," she says, "rather like the idea of that delicious meal. I'd like to take you up on the invitation. I could demolish easily, I think, a *Tafelspitz*. And count me in on the *Kaiserschmarren*."

"Good!" says Miss Thorne. "Come on Edge be a sport!"

Miss Edgely is staring out of the window lurching with every little lurch of the tram. Miss Thorne knowing that she put on the new tartan polyester suit for the first time that day noticed, earlier, Edgely's obvious sense of elation and freedom, as if the trouser suit emancipated her; now, in her dejected state, Edgely draws pity from Miss Thorne.

"Edge!" Miss Thorne says in a voice as low as she can make it, but loud enough to be heard by Edgely over the noise of the tram. "Remind me when we are near a suitable place, I must send a wire to Bales. Before we left I saw a mouse in the Visitors' Room. If it gets into the Edible Art cabinet, the whole display will be ruined. You'll remind me. All right?"

"All right," Miss Edgely says.

"Then it's all settled. Shall we eat at the Hotel Graben?"

They sit in silence. Miss Thorne gives herself up to the swaying movement of the tram,

But jealous souls will not be answered so;
They are not ever jealous for the cause,
But jealous for they are jealous . . .

"Pensive Prickles?"

"Not really Snow, just at work in my head."

Miss Thorne, smiling to herself, thinks of the moment when, after climbing the stairs, she will knock at the door of Gwenda's little room.

Miss Peabody, after receiving the honey and the sheepskins sent by the novelist, simply looked forward with pleasure to all the birthdays.

She was not even depressed about choosing birthday cards; some of them bore the message, "The wording inside this greeting card is Happy Birthday printed in grey." Even that did not sadden her. And, instead of dreading the Fortress Friday Evening party at the New Light Tavern, Miss Peabody was looking forward to it. Though it made her an hour or so later home to her mother, she had started joining in these Friday evening drinks. The next one was special being in the form of a birthday party for Miss Truscott.

I had no trouble, she wrote in her letter to Diana, in deciding which sheepskin to give to Miss Truscott. Naturally I could not give the purple to Mother or to Mrs Brewer. Miss Truscott was ever so pleased with her soft little rug.

83

"Oo!" she said to me, "it'll be ever so cosy by my bed," she said, and then she said, "Oh! you shouldn't have!"

"Oh yes I should have," I said to her, "It's come all the way from Australia for you."

"Thanks ever so much," she said.

For some days Miss Peabody lived on the joy of giving Miss Truscott a gift which was put on view for all the clerks in the outer office. They put their fingers into the fleece, they stroked and patted it.

Had it really come all the way from Australia they wanted to know. It must be real lamb's wool, someone said.

All this made Miss Peabody feel excited and important. It was the same sort of feeling she had had on the day when she had her Blood Pressure to talk about. She felt brave and daring and even cheeky.

"Whew! These stairs! At my age!" she spoke to a junior.

When Mr Bains accused her of having lost an important file, she clasped her head in both hands, saying, "I'd lose my head if it wasn't screwed on!" and felt that she was saying something bright and original.

On the Friday evening, at the party, Miss Peabody found herself wishing that the party was over so that she could get back to her bedroom to continue her letter to Diana.

Tell me about your trees, the novelist asked in the latest letter which had come the day before. I suppose, she wrote, the trees over there are not as tall as our trees. Our Wandoo and Jarrah trees, the Red Gum — Marri, they are called — are very old and grow to great heights.

Dorothy thought about the letter and about her reply. *The magnificent oak tree is the monarch of the English forest* . . . she loved composing fine sentences for her replies. *The magnificent oak tree is the monarch of the English forest* . . . she could hardly wait to write it down. She thought of the hedgerow elms in remote places in the country. Seen from railway carriage windows at sunset, yes, elms were tall trees.

There were other things in the novelist's letter, intimate things. Suggestions and questions. Dorothy longed to answer the letter. She would be home later than usual and would have to make her mother comfortable. Mrs Brewer stayed a little longer on Fridays, but Dorothy would still have all the same things to do before she would be free to write. Always there was the obstacle to be dealt with before she could have time for herself. Undisturbed.

The New Light Tavern, Wild West Ranch Room, was filled with Fortress and Miss Truscott's Birthday Drink celebration.

"What'll you have Miss Peabody?" Mr Bains leaned out from a tight ball of people at the end of the long bar.

"Oh!" Dorothy was ready with her reply, *bitter lemon thank you*, she had rehearsed the little phrase, *I like alcohol but alcohol doesn't like me*, she had prepared another sentence too but instead of saying them she said,

"Brandy and dry, thanks."

"Long?"

"No, short. I don't want it drowned." She hoped others might hear but no one appeared to. She took her drink from the end of Mr Bains' long arm and drank it. Mr Barrington, with prompt chivalry, taking his turn, offered her another which she took. Miss Truscott had her little mulberry over-night bag; it was tucked under the high stool where she sat, as if on a perch, and showing her gun-metalled legs; very firm and shapely legs for her age. Miss Peabody knew that Miss Truscott referred, in general conversation, constantly to the boudoir exercise which kept women over forty trim and neat. A slight bandiness, possibly the result of this exercise, did not embarrass Miss Truscott at all. In fact, she often stood or sat in a particular way so that this crooked shapeliness showed or was even exaggerated. At lunchtime Miss Truscott had declared herself, in the interests of preserving a youthful waistline, to be dedicated henceforth to a diet of oranges.

The Wild West Ranch Room was cloudy with cigarette smoke. The loud rumble of conversation was broken into frequently with shrill laughter. Some people laughed till they coughed and begged their immediate neighbours not to make them laugh so much. Mr Bains was saying that there were no really liberated women. Unmarried ones have a certain freedom he said, but they have to earn a living. Married ones work if they want to but only if husbands are fond enough of money or fond enough of some other woman. There was no such thing, he said, as complete and utter liberation for either women or men. His remarks disappeared in waves of laughter. It was then that Miss Peabody asked,

"How tall are elms, Mr Bains?" blinking up at him through her bifocals. "How tall are elms?" she asked in her brightest and most business-like manner.

Mr Bains told Miss Truscott quietly that he thought Miss Peabody had had too much to drink. Miss Truscott did not feel inclined to take the responsibility but, remembering it was her birthday, she slipped off her stool.

"Would you like to lie down for a bit — dear?" she asked Miss Peabody.

Miss Peabody was not intoxicated, not with one brandy down and one in the hand, but it pleased her immensely to be thought so. She, smiling to people on all sides, allowed Miss Truscott to guide her through the party crowd. It was an unusual moment of glory for Miss Peabody. Already she was thinking ahead to the possible references to it on the following Monday. She lay down on the pink rose chintz chaise longue in the ladies' toilet.

"Better take your shoes off — dear," Miss Truscott covered her with a grey rug which was folded over the end of the chair. "Just you stay there, dear, till you feel better," Miss Truscott said. After doing a few quick things to herself in front of the mirror she rushed back to the party.

In her handbag Miss Peabody had the latest letter from Diana. She had read it. However, being on the long chair seemed a good place to read it once more. She felt self-conscious lying down. In a perky manner she raised her head from the pink rose cushion whenever anyone came in. No one took any notice of her; simply they rushed into the lavatory and, after making a lot of noise, rushed out again. Miss Peabody always went to the lavatory quietly herself.

There was an odd page in the letter. It did not seem to fit in with Miss Thorne or Miss Edgely at all. Diana had written once before saying that she sometimes wrote things in the wrong order, or that things came in to the writing which were irrelevant for the reader but necessary for the writer.

Since this last operation, the page of the novelist's letter was typed. This in itself was unusual but Miss Peabody was ready to accept anything from Diana Hopewell. There was no doubt in her mind, there would be a slot somewhere at some time for this page.

"For every pot there is a lid," Miss Peabody, lying down on the chaise longue in the Ladies of the New Light Tavern, uttered one of Mrs Brewer' wise sayings. Lifting her head in the same perky manner she giggled. No one was there to see her. She reread the page, having forgotten from the day before exactly what was on it.

Since this last operation, the typing was flawless, I am practically helpless. After the hip replacement two years ago I was incapacitated for almost six months because of the diathermy burn on my right thigh. Naturally I could not sue the hospital for damages because I cannot antagonize people when I depend on them. I am a patient, well a prisoner really, in Ward A several times a year as you know. Furthermore you will remember that all the equipment used was destroyed immediately so there was no evidence. You, of course, were not available as you were abroad. I would like to say here that you are never available, because of holidays, during those critical weeks following one of the big, as you call them, prophylactic operations.

Now, the knee joint operations have been a disaster. I am

entirely unable to bend the knees. It is impossible for me to dress myself and impossible for me to get into the car, let alone drive it. And I would like to know what has been done to my feet. Is it possible that you have cut all the tendons to my toes? I find walking impossible. I cannot buy shoes or slippers to fit on my now deformed feet.

It seems to me that you are too eager to operate always round Christmas time.

> . . . brought many captives home to Rome
> whose ransoms did the general coffers fill . . .

That is a quotation from Shakespeare but I do not expect you to know this. You are keen on surgery but the condition of the patient afterwards does not really concern you. You are not in the least interested in the results of your surgery. In fact on every occasion, following surgery, when I have needed a consultation you have been away, either on your yacht or somewhere in Europe.

I want you to know that after every operation which you tell me I must have, and I expect there are others in the same predicament, I am older and frailer and less able to do anything for myself. I am considerably poorer too.

Congratulate yourself, dear sir, on increasing the number of helpless cripples in our community.

Fortunately for me my illness has not attacked either my hands or my brain. I intend, in the future, to keep both my hands and my head well away from you. I intend to return to my farm and shut

Here the page of typing ended and the next page, after the part about the trees, went straight on with Miss Thorne climbing the stairs in the Pension eagerly going towards the door of Gwenda's little room.

Miss Peabody, having recovered from the idea of the effects of the brandy, thought she would go home. It would be a good chance to try the art of navigation. She would navigate the sky. Diana, the Goddess of the Hunt, knew the way home by the tree tops. The paths of the sky lay between the tossing foliage.

The evening was light and fragrant and warm. A fine sprinkling shower had dampened the dust and the pavements were shining. The green leaves of early summer pressing behind railings and the fresh smell of the rain on the dust excited Miss Peabody. It should be possible to find her way to Kingston Avenue quite easily, after all, the train ride was not so terribly long. The evenings stayed light now for some hours.

There did not seem to be many people in the streets and she had no idea who the man was. He was well spoken, polite, with kind accents and a gentle tone.

"Do you think you should have a taxi, madam?" Miss Peabody could not see him very well. Looking up at the sky had, as before, caused her hat to fall crookedly over her spectacles.

"Shall I? Do you think you should have a taxi?" Miss Peabody heard his voice near and then far away. She smiled. "I think I should have had more watter with it." She giggled and collapsed against the railings. "Itsho funny!" she said, "what we need are some ellems in a shedge jus' to sho ush the way, to sho ush the harbush in the shky. Excushe me! are ellems tall?" she hiccupped and peered up at the stranger.

"Oh!" she gasped, realizing with horror, "the Pollish! The Pollish!"

"Oh! Parties! Parties! I am in a Bad Mood!" Miss Peabody told everyone in the main office at Fortress on the following Monday morning. "I like alcohole but alcohole doesn't like me," she sang, "I should have had more water with it," she said and looked round at the other desks and tables. "I'm in a Really Bad Mood!" she announced. The typewriters, the addressing machines and the adding up machines were all rattling away and no one even looked in Miss Peabody's direction.

It was clear when Miss Truscott emerged from the sanctuary of the inner office that the weekend had not been all it should have been. Miss Truscott was in a bad mood and this could not be ignored. Feeling hurt because no one had asked her how and when she had arrived home on Friday night, Miss Peabody said crossly into the noise of the busy office,

"Don't disturb me. I've got more to do than to just chat!"

There is no reply when Miss Thorne, after mounting the stairs, knocks at the door of Gwenda's little room, Miss Peabody began to reread the novelist's letter late in the evening after what turned out to be a sour and tedious day. Miss Truscott had not spoken to her and she, in her turn, had wordlessly walked up to Miss Truscott and, after thrusting some papers into her unwilling hands, had turned away, stumping woodenly back to her own place.

As she read she began to feel better. She ignored the typed page, something about an operation. Probably it would fall into place. She read on, her mother asleep at last; the night belonged to the novelist.

Miss Thorne is more than a little out of breath, not just from the stairs, it is something else; it is a curious and disquieting stirring of an excitement. She is perplexed that within her sixty year old breast there is this excitement. During the last part of the tram ride, returning from Grinzing, Miss Thorne composed a short biography of Richard Wagner for Gwenda. (Only in her head of course.)

When roused to speak of something that interested him he looked what he meant and his rich voice gave a musical effect to his words. She remembers reading this about Wagner and feels it would be a good way to introduce the student to the composer before

90

going on to some details about the music. She is hoping to take Gwenda to Bayreuth next year and, in her mind, is the determination to include Debbie Frome. The idea came to her, like an inspiration, in the tram; Mr Frome could easily provide the money for this hitherto unthought-of culture for Debbie.

She knocks again at the varnished door. It is strange, she thinks, that there is no answer. Perhaps the gel is asleep, the thought is touching. She opens the door. The tiny room is very tidy as would be expected from someone reared at Pine Heights. It is empty.

Possibly Gwenda is still in the garden, in one of the lilac scented arbours. The evening is light and warm.

Miss Thorne hurries down the passage to the big room.

"Betty's gone to the bathroom," Miss Edgely says, speaking very quickly.

"I don't mind where Snow is. Have you seen Gwenda?"

"Yes," says Miss Edgely, head down, fussing through her case. "She was here a moment ago. I found her in here searching for something. She said she was looking for a stamp. She needed stamps, she said. She wondered if we had any. She'd pulled a few things about," Miss Edgely adds, indicating the dressing table cloth which has been pulled off. Miss Thorne notices at once that her letter is missing.

"I told her she could buy stamps at the tobacconist's on the corner," Miss Edgely says, still busy with the clothes in her suitcase.

"But Edge, you can't have let the gel go out on her own." Miss Thorne feels a mixture of anxiety and anger rising somewhere inside her. "Edge! The gel can hardly speak a word of German and here, in Vienna, it's much harder to understand people. How could you send her out! Anything might happen!"

"I didn't think she should be in our room . . . " Miss Edgely starts to speak.

"You didn't think!"

"What's the trouble, Prickles?" Miss Snowdon, drying her hands on a small towel, comes in.

Miss Thorne hurries from the room and along the passage and down the stairs to the street. She is tired after the day and very worried.

There is no sign of Gwenda in the crowded street. The woman in the kiosk says that many people have purchased stamps, magazines, newspapers, cigarettes — everything. She does not recollect a fair haired schoolgirl.

The lilac tosses over empty arbours and Miss Thorne hurries back upstairs to the big room where she gives Miss Edgely a good shaking.

"I say Prickles! Prickles deah! Don't Prickles. Her head will fall orf!" Miss Snowdon puts a warning hand on Miss Thorne's quivering shoulder.

"Snow! we'll have to go out and search for Gwenda."

"But Prickles, she's only been gorn a few minutes. The gel's not an absolute fool. She's probably looking in shop windows and will be back soon."

"I'm sorry Edge!" Miss Thorne sees the sense in Miss Snowdon's words. "Sorry! Simply forgot myself for a moment," she tries to shake hands with Miss Edgely. "We'll wash and change shall we?" she says, "remember I am taking you all to the Hotel Graben this evening."

Miss Thorne tries to overcome the disturbance she feels about Gwenda being out alone. Apart from her own feeling for Gwenda, she is responsible for her. Mr Manners, it is true, has left Gwenda, but Miss Thorne knows from previous experience that such parents react more strongly in the event of an emergency which involves their child. It is clear that Gwenda has taken the letter which was addressed to her. There was nothing wrong with the letter she tells herself, but it would have been better to talk. She is uncomfortable with the thought that Gwenda was in their room. And, that she took something, the letter, is an uncomfortable thing too. Perhaps she has taken something else. Miss

Thorne feels unhappy about it.

Gwenda does not return. Instead of going out for the promised meal, they sit down, uneasily, to the evening soup
offered at the Pension. The younger of the two ladies Eppelseimer agrees that it is a matter for the police, especially as
Miss Edgely, after the shaking is too upset to eat and has
gone out against Miss Thorne's advice to look for Gwenda.

"First left, second right and right again," Miss Snowdon
and Miss Thorne are walking the streets, the brightly lit main
thoroughfares and the little dark side streets and alleys. It
seems pointless to go on walking. They return to the Pension
to wait.

"I'm so terribly worried Snow."

"Yes Prickles, of course we both are. But they are bound
to turn up. People don't just disappear."

"But Snow, remember we are in Europe. God! What if
Gwenda . . . "

"Hush Prickles! Such thoughts are unprofitable."

"And then there's Edge. You know, she was really hurt
when I, you know, sort of, well, shook her."

"Ah well, she deserved it no doubt."

"She-ah, she took a good pull at her brandy, that worries
me too."

"There's a special providence, Prickles, which looks after
drunks and children — so what else do we need?"

"Oh! if only that was true!"

Miss Edgely is asleep at the police station. She is in a clean
lock-up cell on a bunk which is like a shelf fastened by chains
to the wall. Someone has covered her with a grey blanket.
The police officer takes Miss Thorne first to identify Miss
Edgely and then into the next neat lock-up cell where
Gwenda is sitting, bloodstained, on a chair. A stout woman,

in police uniform, is sitting on a chair beside her. She is trying to talk to Gwenda with one or two words of English.
Miss Thorne, disgusted with the sight and sound of Miss
Edgely, almost cries when she sees Gwenda whose white
stockings are covered in blood. Her summer frock too is
stained.

"Are you hurt Gwenda deah?" Miss Thorne has no room
to rush forward. She fills up the cell. "Whatever happened to
you, deah gel? I've been so worried!"

Gwenda smiles at Miss Thorne. She is relieved and pleased
to see her. She does not seem frightened.

"I'm sorry Miss Thorne. I went for a walk this afternoon
and lost the way. I kept thinking I was going in the right
direction and all the time I must have been going farther and
farther along the wrong way!"

"But all that blood deah?"

The police woman smiles, "Is only," she consults a
battered phrase book, "is *ihre* — her, *ihre Monatsfluss*, is her
menses? *Ich*, I, fix her, how you say, fix up?" She pats her
own pubic region in explanation.

Miss Thorne nods. There is nothing romantic or dangerous
after all. She is used to dealing with girls and problems of this
nature, though never in a police station. She smiles at
Gwenda, misquoting in her head,

". . . who would have thought, there could be so much
blood . . . Shakespeare."

"A good hot bath and some hot milk and then bed," Miss
Thorne says to Gwenda, "and you can relate your adventures tomorrow, on the morrow." They are squeezed into the
back of a taxi. Miss Edgely, who has been violently sick, is
asleep again, her head rolling from side to side rests on Miss
Thorne's shoulder and bumps off only to rest there again.

Later, in the spacious room when Miss Thorne has been
along the passage to say good night to Gwenda, they, Miss
Snowdon, Miss Thorne and Miss Edgely put their mattresses

in a row on the floor. After such an experience there is a great deal of consoling to be done.

"*ihm wurden zwei Pferde unter dem Leibe getötet — he had two horses killed under him.*"

"Still working Prickles?"

"Yes, I suppose so, Snow, only in my head you know. I must teach Gwenda some German. I was simply working out a phrase for 'had' d'you see."

"A good example Prickles."

"Thank you Snow."

"Good night deah."

"Good night."

Travelling, Miss Thorne reflects in the darkness, causes many irregularities. Gwenda, at the gentle reproach for allowing herself to be taken unawares by her own normal functions, explained,

"But it's not meant to come for another week, Miss Thorne."

"Of course deah, it's the travelling." Miss Thorne is sorry about reproaching her for carelessness.

Gwenda has not said anything about the letter and Miss Thorne has not asked her. When she said,

"Tomorrow we must buy stamps for your postcards, Gwenda," the girl, sitting in bed with her glass of hot milk, replied,

"Oh yes please, Miss Thorne. I've written at least twelve cards and three letters."

"Including one to your father, deah?"

"Yes, six pages."

"Good gel!"

Perhaps Edge was mistaken. Uneasily Miss Thorne can see for herself that her own letter is not where she put it.

Miss Thorne, always the last to fall asleep, thinks of other things too. Gwenda's flooding, as the girls at Pine Heights would call it, is an indication of her youth and the purpose of her body to which Miss Thorne knows she has no right. For the first time she experiences a slight heartache, perhaps it is more than slight. She tries, sleepless, to dismiss it. She knows she is being ridiculous. Perhaps travelling is upsetting her too though naturally not in the same way. Miss Edgely has already had difficulties of a different kind and has had a row of little enamel jugs of hot water brought to her on a tray on two mornings. Miss Thorne does not wish to have the hot water jugs brought in such a public way. She hopes she may avoid them. In a few days they will leave for London. She does not feel able to send Gwenda back alone to Pine Heights. Perhaps Edge will soften and they will travel together to England.

As soon as they arrive home, just after the beginning of term, the three junior mistresses will have to go. Bad to let them start the term but there is no other way. These thoughts travel monotonously through her mind in that pattern of thinking which precedes sleep. Suddenly she is fully awake with a flash of understanding. If Gwenda went for a walk and lost the way then she could not have been in their room when they returned from Grinzing. While Miss Thorne went to knock at Gwenda's door, Miss Snowdon went straight to the lavatory and Miss Edgely was the first to go into their big room.

Miss Thorne cautiously caressing the sleeping Miss Edgely's breast gently removes from the inside of her nightgown the letter. Her own letter to Gwenda carefully folded and tucked into that faithful and ancient hiding place. She is surprised that she did not feel it there earlier. Miss Edgely, possibly because of the need to conceal the letter, has gone to bed wearing various articles of underclothing under her nightgown.

"Prickles deah, can you lie still?"

"Sorry, sorry Snow."

"That's all right Prickles, no harm meant. Still working I suppose."

"Not really, nothing much, but good night deah."

"Good night Prickles."

Still sleep eludes Miss Thorne. Gwenda's *Monatsfluss*, what a splendid name, almost poetic, monthly flow, however, sounds definitely working class. Gwenda's menstruation so purposeful and plentiful is an indication of her natural independence. For a moment Miss Thorne wishes Gwenda to be pregnant and abandoned so that she, Miss Thorne, could take her to herself and look after her.

Miss Peabody, on her way home from the station, called in at the local public library and asked for a book on Wagner. She had been rereading the letters from the novelist. She knew nothing about Wagner and his life and his music.

"*The* Ring of the Nibelung," she read, "*is both the noblest and the hugest work ever attempted by the creative mind. It really comprises four music dramas. It was a Herculean achievement, the fulfilment of which required the energy, imagination, and horizon of a man who had in him a touch of something more than human.*" Miss Peabody sighed about all the foreign names. She thought about the chops she would fry, a special treat for her mother. She tried to read on, skipping the names, "*The individual tragedy of one is related to the tragedy of another and both are subordinated to the tragedy of the world that is their undoing;*" Miss Peabody, unable to understand completely, returned the book.

"So many Rings," she said, "it confuses me. I'll read it another time," she said to the librarian. She hurried home, "The individual tragedy of one is related to the tragedy of another," the words, for some reason, reminded her of Miss Thorne and Miss Edgely.

At the end of her last letter the novelist had written about yet another composer also unknown to Miss Peabody.

I wonder if you know the *German Requiem* of Brahms?

Diana, as she often did, had written a flamboyant postscript which covered an extra page. There is a part, she wrote, which I love very much: "*Ihr habt nun Traurigkeit*". It comes after the chorus, "How Lovely Is Thy Dwelling Place", or more correctly, from Psalm 84, "How amiable are thy tabernacles O Lord of Hosts!" Well, after that, the soprano sings, "*Ihr habt nun Traurigkeit*," which in English is, "And, ye who now therefore have sorrow: but I will see you again, and your heart shall rejoice, and your joy no man taketh from you." It's from St John Chapter 16 Verse 22 and the voice rises with the music. It's superb! I'd like it played when I die. After I am dead, at my funeral, I would like this played. D'you see, I want the soprano voice to go with me wherever I go. The soprano sings over the tops of the tossing trees, through the restless foliage and up over the sunlit tree tops for miles on and up. The voice is sweet and tender and, at the same time, sure and sustained. It's lovely music. When I'm on my way home I think of this music above the trees. It comes from behind the shining edges of the clouds. It's as if I hear it in the noise of the wind.

Miss Peabody was moved. Diana wrote so well, and she, Dorothy Peabody, was insignificant yet receiving these intimate details of the famous novelist's life. She knew that now in May, if the expected and hoped for rain had come, it would be the time for seeding. No doubt Diana was out on horseback supervising the sowing of her paddocks. Perhaps, with some indescribable machinery, she was doing the work herself.

Miss Peabody's evenings had become another world. A world of magic and enchantment. She lived for the evenings and for the time spent with the novelist's letters and the composing of her own replies.

All the different things her mother asked for hardly mattered. The petulant voice calling down the narrow stairs could not remove the anticipation of her happiness.

"Dotty! Dotty! Mrs Brewer, can you hear me Dotty? Mrs

Brewer fancies anchovies in her lunch. Anchovy Dotty! Dotty! Tomorrow! Anchovy! Brewer!"

"Righty-O mother. Anchovy."

"Dotty! Dotty! You've not dusted the piano again I never heard you dust the piano. Dotty! The piano! Dotty!"

"Righty-O mother. I'm just in the front room now. I'm on the piano now mother."

Paddocks was a wonderful word for fields. Diana's paddocks, with neat chocolate coloured ridges of fresh ploughed earth, would stretch to the horizon. Diana had once written that the parched land turned green overnight with just one shower of rain. A faint mist of fresh green showing on the brown earth, Dorothy tried to imagine it.

Every Friday night, even though it meant being later home to her mother, Miss Peabody went to the Wild West Ranch Room of the New Light Tavern for a Friday drink with Fortress. She bought gun-metal pantyhose like Miss Truscott's, not exactly the "gun-metal" colour because it would not do to imitate too closely. She chose "steel" and tried to sit or stand so that her legs, which were quite bandy enough, looked as much as possible like Miss Truscott's fleshless but shapely legs. The "steel" stockings gleamed in the New Light. Miss Peabody ordered brandy and dry. Later blinking behind her round glasses, looking at herself in the mirror in the ladies' toilet she thought she looked pleasantly cheeky.

At last sitting at her shabby dressing table she could read the latest letter from Diana. She could read slowly and slowly she could start her reply. Looking forward to composing and writing her reply had become for her the greatest pleasure she had ever known.

She thought, if she tried, she would hear the soprano voice, tender and sweet, above the trees in the park. It was simply a matter of remembering to walk through the park; the little park would not make the walk to the station so much longer. In her lunchtime she could walk in the park in

London; it was something she would make a point of doing.

There was a tremendous excitement in knowing that they, Miss Thorne and Miss Edgely and Gwenda would, quite soon, all be in London. It was not impossible that, knowing what she knew, she might meet them, run into them perhaps by chance especially if she took a walk in one of the big parks.

She could look forward to writing more of her letter the next night. She would, later, lie in bed with her window open to the summer night fragrance of the small suburban gardens. She would, in the dark, reach out to Diana and Diana would enfold her. But first there was the letter to read.

Somewhere between Vienna and Paris Miss Edgely gets left behind in a station lavatory, the novelist's letter started straight in without any enquiries or remarks of a personal kind.

"D'you think I've got time?" Miss Edgely asks.

"Oh, rather! Edge of course you have, but don't be all day." Miss Thorne notices that the guards are slamming the doors of the Express. All round them are the noises of departure. She knows Miss Edgely has not really time. Whistles blow and flags wave.

It is one of the big stations where trains are continually arriving and leaving. Announcements of arrival and departure are made in several languages and beneath the station clock people wait to be met or to be forgotten.

"It's too bad," Miss Thorne murmurs, "Miss Edgely has missed the train."

Gwenda, opposite, is smiling.

"Are you keeping your diary up to date?" Miss Thorne returns the smile. "You will have to write your impressions of the famous *Ring*. Let me see," Miss Thorne studies

Gwenda's face, "Can you remember all the names?" She is enjoying the rhythm of the railway.

"*Stubenring*," Gwenda says.

"Ah yes, *Park Ring*," Miss Thorne says, "let me see, *Schubert Ring* and *Kärntner Ring*."

"*Opern Ring*," Gwenda says. Miss Thorne says yes and repeats the name to correct Gwenda's pronounciation.

"*Burgring*," she says after a little pause.

"*Karl-Renner Ring*," Gwenda says.

"And there's one more," Miss Thorne, laughing, tries to think, "one more and then *Schotten Ring*."

"Wedding Ring," Gwenda says. They both laugh.

"When we are in London," Miss Thorne is serious again, "you must write up all your adventures."

"I will," Gwenda says.

Miss Edgely arrives at the hotel in London a day late. Miss Snowdon, whose holiday is over, has returned to her hospital.

The hotel is drab and in a not so good part of London. Miss Thorne feels that as it is cheaper there one can spend money, without troubling the conscience too much, on the revival of Oscar Wilde. There are a series of matinee performances in a once handsome theatre where afternoon tea is brought during the intervals in little silver tea pots with china cups and slices of dark fruit cake by waitresses, with exquisite balance, in tight black dresses smelling slightly of perspiration. Gwenda finds the maids' uniforms amusing, in particular the tiny useless white aprons and the caps, threaded with black ribbon, worn low on the forehead. Their clothes, like the play, belong to another world. They are a part of the revival Miss Thorne explains.

They have afternoon tea again, this time in deep armchairs

watching well trained maidens as they parade to and fro wearing the fine woollen fashions for the next winter.

"Winter woollies!" Miss Edgely fans herself with the programme, "and it's not the end of May!"

The girls, anticipating autumn with delicate russet colours, walk forward three long steps and, turning round, they stand, legs apart, swinging a skirt, pulling off a cloak, tossing back a scarf and then they turn again as if opening and offering themselves momentarily to the contented audience before swinging off with more long competent strides to make room for yet another group of girls in different clothes.

"Children liked to be near him," Miss Thorne flushed with fashions and hot tea leans forward. She is describing Wagner's physical appearance to Gwenda, "for your scrapbook, Gwenda, we shall buy a postcard of the von Lenbach portrait, and, very neatly, you can write in a paragraph of description. He loved rich colours," she continues, "he loved fine clothes and good food. He liked unusual furniture and pictures. He carried himself well," Miss Thorne straightens her own back as well as she is able in the deep soft armchair. "Though he was unconventional, he was a man with refined taste," she laughs; the subject excites her and she likes to talk to Gwenda. "He was slightly under middle height," she says, "but because of his forcefulness, he seemed taller. His movements were quick and so was his speech. Somewhere, I read a description of his clothes, an overcoat of dark green buckskin, a velvet waistcoat — very romantic — a silk neckerchief, a felt hat and . . . "

"Well!" says Miss Edgely, "if that isn't Debbie Frome over there."

"Where deah?" Miss Thorne is used to Miss Edgely's short sight making mistakes.

"There, just across there, watching the mannequins like us."

As we are, Miss Thorne corrects Miss Edgely in her head and looks, with narrowed eyes, at the little round tables and the semicircles of armchairs.

"The man with her looks old enough to be her father, that man biting into the chocolate eclair." Miss Edgely, bored with Wagner and even more bored with Gwenda, is glad of an interruption.

"Oh so it is. That is her father." Miss Thorne notices that Gwenda's face, which is usually pale, is suddenly pink.

"Do you wish to go over and speak to Debbie?" Miss Thorne sees a chance for the hoped for friendship between the two girls. Gwenda starts to rise from her chair. She is slow and shy. But Debbie is quickly beside them, her bright eyes peering through the long fringe. Her feet are neat in expensive, narrow-strapped Italian sandals. Miss Thorne cannot help noticing that her toenails are a startling vermillion colour. She refrains from telling the gel that her toes are the height of vulgarity.

"Well," says Debbie before anyone can speak, "where you all spring from? You could a knocked us down with a feather! Lovely to see you. Where you stayin' then?"

Miss Thorne has hardly time to flinch at the gel's speech.

"Good afternoon!" Mr Frome is standing beside their chairs. "Good afternoon ladies!" He is polite in his north of England accent and some new clothes. He is wearing a crisp woollen, brown and fawn checked jacket, and trousers of soft, dark brown suede. Miss Thorne remembers Mr Frome as a short man, anxious about his only daughter; here he seems tall. Even if a little fleshy round the neck and the nose he cuts a dashing figure she observes to herself, critical in her mind about the cliché "dashing figure" but feeling that it fits.

"If you ladies are comfy in them chairs," Mr Frome says when the formal exclamations of surprise and pleasure are over, " 'ow would't be if Miss Gwenda here comes with our Deb just now. She can't make up 'er mind over a dress I said I'd buy her — if she wanted it, we'll be no more than half an hour. She's had't on three times and, like a woman, keeps changin' mind. A second opinion, like, from the female sex would work wonders I don't doubt!" He winks at Miss Thorne who is surprised.

"Why of course!" Miss Thorne takes care not to show that she is surprised. "Miss Edgely and I will be perfectly comfortable here till you come back. You would like to go Gwenda?"

Edgely dozes in her chair. Miss Thorne goes through, in her mind, the possibilities. It is as though Mr Frome has fallen from the ordinary Frome routine of living and round of pleasure straight into her lap. Perhaps during the few days in London a friendship between Gwenda and Debbie can be established. Miss Thorne, still flushed, feels satisfied and luxurious in the deep round armchair. Her eyes gleam. The hollow cheque from Mr Manners scarcely seems to matter now. There will be ways and means, she nods, reasoning to herself. Bayreuth with both girls is a very happy thought and a very possible one. She can start at once to prepare them for the season next year.

"Did you make a mistake then Gwenda?" Miss Thorne is in Gwenda's room in the hotel. They are about to leave with Miss Edgely, who is not quite ready, to join Mr Frome and Debbie for an evening meal at Frome's Hotel. Mr Frome's sister-in-law, Violet, is the manageress, he explained to Miss Thorne as they were leaving the fashion floor of the department store. He offered to call for them.

"Certainly not, but thank you all the same," Miss Thorne, smiling, said, "it is not far, it is quite within walking distance. We shall enjoy the walk."

"The best cook in London is our Vi," Mr Frome assured his future guests. "You'd do well t' move traps and stop there. It's nought much of a district and nought much to look at but place has all t' comforts o' home." He told them he always stayed there himself when he was in England before going north to Bradford to see his mother.

"Debbie's grandma, a right proper one she is! We're off up there day after tomorrow for a day or two before we go back down-under. There's School," Mr Frome added, "and there's my business."

Miss Thorne accepted his invitation with a readiness which took her by surprise. She is disappointed that they will lose Debbie and Mr Frome so quickly. The meeting, the invitation, her own happiness about these, and something else, has made the whole day one of surprises.

"Did you make a mistake then Gwenda?" Miss Thorne asks again speaking gently. Her feeling is one of anger following surprise. She carefully conceals the anger and makes her voice as gentle and tender as she can.

"Did you make a mistake then Gwenda when you chose a present and, after making the mistake, not like to say to Mr Frome that you had made a mistake? I am sure it can be changed for something else."

"Oh No, it's quite all right Miss Thorne, it's what I wanted. Really, I chose it. I want to keep it. Please!"

"Are you perfectly sure Gwenda," Miss Thorne is, without wanting to appear to be, more severe. "I mean, he offered you a new dress. You could have chosen a dress. He said that he loved shopping. He said that you had helped Debbie to make up her mind. He wanted to buy you something really nice, those were his words. That is what he said."

"Debbie had really made up her mind Miss Thorne, I didn't really do anything. She had already made up her mind." Gwenda has her present from Mr Frome's little shopping expedition spread out on her bed. Miss Thorne can hardly bring herself to look at it.

"I really want this Miss Thorne. It's what I really want. You don't mind do you?"

"No, of course not Gwenda, you know I would never

mind." Miss Thorne is tender once more. She will have to watch over Gwenda carefully. She realizes more and more how vulnerable she is. "Well you had better pack it away. It's rather bulky. Such things usually are." She laughs awkwardly as Gwenda slowly assembles and puts away the extraordinary present she has chosen.

.

"I'm tickled pink!" Mr Frome enjoys his meal. Violet Frome is pleased to meet Miss Thorne and Miss Edgely and Gwenda. The table, with a white cloth and sauce bottles and a gigantic cruet is in the bay window.

Mr Frome and Debbie and their visitors are the only guests in for the high tea. They have the dining room to themselves and they can watch the desultory activities of the city back street. The evening is light and warm.

"She's a lovely lass!" Mr Frome admires Gwenda as she goes with Debbie to the sideboard to fetch what Violet calls the sweets, little glass dishes containing custards of various colours sprinkled with dessicated coconut and decorated with glacé cherries, red ones and green. "She's bonny that lass! She's a big girl," he says with approval.

"Yes," Miss Thorne murmurs, her mind elsewhere. Mr Frome looks after Miss Edgely. He makes a fuss of her, sending his sister-in-law for brandy when he finds out, which he does quite quickly, that it is her drink.

Debbie Frome is wearing the new dress. It is in perfect taste. Miss Thorne can see that it is expensive. The good quality is apparent first in the colour, a delicate mushroom colour; then in the material, a very fine wool, exquisitely knitted; it is almost like fine lace. And, of course, it fits Debbie perfectly.

Miss Thorne cannot help wishing, as she sits there, that Gwenda had chosen a dress when she had the chance. It is not that one should grab, Miss Thorne thinks to herself, but that when an opportunity presents itself, it is so important to make the best use of it. Gwenda really needs a sophisticated dress like Debbie's.

Mr Frome sends Debbie upstairs for her cassette player. "Let's have a bit o' music," he says.

The girls are dancing. Debbie is teaching Gwenda the steps. Mr Frome, contented, is leaning back with his cigar. Miss Edgely has a second brandy. Miss Thorne wishes that Miss Snowdon had accompanied them to London. She needs to discuss with her the strange choice Gwenda made when she was asked to choose something as a gift from Mr Frome.

"I'm tickled pink!" Mr Frome is unable to take his eyes off Gwenda. "She's a lovely lass! How did you like the parkin?"

"I beg your pardon?" Miss Edgely giggles.

"Mr Frome means the treacle cake," Miss Thorne explains to Miss Edgely, "it's called Yorkshire Parkin, you had a piece with your coffee," she gives Edgely a stern look.

"It was delicious, thank you," Miss Thorne smiles at Mr Frome who is giving off a warmth, an aura of well being brought about by an abundance of money, good food, good clothes, property in more countries than one, a boat, two or three Rover cars and various successful deals in his many adventures in business. Miss Thorne feels as if she is sunbathing in this warmth. It is almost as if she is being admired by Mr Frome. She enjoys this feeling too.

Mr Frome drinks a large cup of sweet tea.

"Me an Debbie we've been livin it up the last few days," Mr Frome says uncrossing his short legs and recrossing them. "I've always liked London. We've just been muckin' about, doin' anything as we felt like doing."

"How splendid!" Miss Thorne says.

They watch the girls dancing.

"Dancin' girls laid on!" Mr Frome claps his hands and taps his foot as the girls dance to and fro across the room, arms loose, heads jerking and hips rolling. Gwenda, Miss Thorne notices with pleasure, seems to be understanding the movements of the dance. Even if it is a little vulgar, she tells herself, one must move with the times — for Gwenda's sake. She thinks, with tenderness, of the shiny card Gwenda has chosen for her and the loving message she has written inside,

For my Best Friend. I would do

anything in the world for you. Gwenda

She knows she should not encourage Gwenda in this devotion. She knows too that her own feelings should not be encouraged. This evening, however, Miss Thorne allows herself, without constraint, to watch Gwenda and her pleasant clumsy body as she attempts to imitate and learn what Debbie can do so easily. Mr Frome's relaxed happiness is pleasant and Miss Thorne allows herself to enjoy this too.

"She's a big girl." Mr Frome is still looking at Gwenda. "I offered her a dress. There was a nice one. Deb said t'were her size. 'No thank you Mr Frome,' she said, 'No thank you Mr Frome,'" he laughs. "Dress were fine stuff," he makes a small movement with his thumb and finger as if feeling and sizing up the quality of cloth. "Light grey and darker grey narrow stripe wi' just a hint o' silver. Very nice for a blonde, the grey with blue tints and the shots o' silver. Stripes just enough that you could see they was stripes going up and down as so they should on a big girl."

"You seem to know a great deal about clothes," Miss Thorne says.

"Anything that's my business I make a point of knowing about. Know your products, know your market, know your customers. Well, there's yourself. Take the school. Pine Tree . . . "

"Pine Heights," Miss Thorne corrects Mr Frome, "is not a business. Pine Heights is, above all, a warm, caring, supporting environment — a background of culture — "

"Anything that gets you bread and butter and rags on your back is a business." Mr Frome leans back in his cloud of cigar smoke. Miss Thorne reflects on the truth of what has just been said. She wonders if this would be the right time to confide in Mr Frome and tell him some of the financial problems and some of the ideas for improvements she has.

"I hope, I mean, I can see that Debbie is very happy at Pine Heights," Miss Thorne says with a pleasant tone in her voice. Miss Edgely is coughing.

"Oh sorry! sorry Girlie!" Mr Frome says, "I'll throw the noxious weed out. Here, our Deb, run off out t' back wi' this," he gives her the end of his cigar, "and get our Violet to bring us another cup." He holds out his tea cup, it is big and decorated with "Father" in gold writing.

"You know," he leans towards Miss Thorne, "something's come over me tonight. I'm really happy t'night."

"I am so glad," Miss Thorne, arching her brows, gives one of her more charming smiles.

"I'm just tickled pink about young Gwenda and what she chose for a present. She's showed it you I suppose?"

"Yes, she has."

"It's just what I would have liked her to choose though I would never'a thought of it till she picked her choice. I wanted for her to have the dress as well. I've always liked to see a woman in something pretty. But could I get her to take the dress!" he pauses, "here y'are Girlie," he helps Miss Edgely who is trying to pour herself a third and generous brandy. "Now ladies what is it to be tonight — Bingo, Bowling or the Dogs?"

"Dogs?" Miss Thorne does not understand.

"Greyhound racing."

"Oh I see. Oh I don't think . . . "

"Aw come on Miss Thorne, it's good fun! We'll go in the Rover eh dad?" Debbie Frome grins. "Dad's changed his image, he used to have a Cadillac, now he's got this black Rover. A 1968 model. Talk about comfy!"

"Aye, fancy meself as a brewer's wife," Mr Frome laughs, "car's supposed to have belonged to such, one owner stuff, only driven to church, there's a prayer book in the glove box to prove it!" he laughs. "Deb, show them where the bathroom is and then we're off."

Late that night Miss Thorne taps at the door of Gwenda's room,

"May I come in Gwenda?" she opens the door, "to say 'good night'."

"Of course Miss Thorne," Gwenda's clothes are folded neatly, she has on her nightdress.

"Ah! there's the present!" Miss Thorne sees the chosen gift, its various parts spread on the bed.

"Yes, I was just looking at all the things," Gwenda says, "look there's even a little washable cuddly toy, do you think it's a rabbit?"

"Heavens! it could be anything." Miss Thorne examines the little stuffed animal, "being pink, I suppose it doesn't really matter," awkwardly she replaces the toy.

"It goes in here," Gwenda quickly intercepts the placing of the little animal, indicating a special pocket in the bag, "next to the feeding bottle, see, there are pockets for two feeding bottles, and the little bundle of napkins fits in here — and this part, lined with plastic, is for used nappies. And there's a tiny hair brush and a little towel and a special pocket for cotton wool and there's even a tube of baby cream . . . "

"Gwenda," Miss Thorne's tone is deep and she sings the name, "Gwenda."

Gwenda looks up.

"Is anything the matter Miss Thorne?"

"No of course not, but perhaps you should pack this all away. You see deah, it's much too soon to be, er, well, collecting something like this . . . "

She watches the girl as all the things are quickly and neatly repacked into the bag. It is spacious and made of plastic covered with pink and blue golliwogs. It closes at the top with an efficient zip.

"I really love it," Gwenda says, tucking in the pink rabbit. "I can keep it till, well, till a time when I will use it, can't I?"

"Yes of course you can, but that time is still quite a long time ahead. You still have your career to consider." Miss Thorne, remembering the recent marriage of Mr Manners, pauses, there might well not be funds for a career. "I mean," she adds, "we all have to learn to earn our crust deah."

"Oh yes, I know," Gwenda says. She is clutching the bag by its coloured handles and swinging it. She looks down at it. "I can just see myself arriving somewhere with this bag, you know, how mothers do."

Miss Thorne says yes she is sure mothers do arrive and they do have bags full of all the things their babies are likely to need. It has never belonged to her own life but she acknowledges it with a gentle inclination of her head.

"There were albums there," Gwenda continues, the memory excites her. "Oh Miss Thorne, I couldn't decide which to choose, the bag or the album. The album was lovely too, Miss Thorne, with spaces for round photographs and oval ones. There were some pages for keeping records of dates and baby's weight, and there were little poems written out to fit with time passing, you know, three months, six months, the first birthday . . . "

"I am sure Mr Frome is a very kind and a very generous man," Miss Thorne feels her energy returning as she speaks of him, "if you had said you wanted an album as well, he would have been happy to buy it. After all, his idea was to give you a dress like Debbie."

"But why!" Gwenda cries out, "why should he want to buy someone like me anything. I felt awkward about choosing a present. I simply felt I couldn't accept the expensive dress. But when I saw this bag I couldn't resist it, so I asked for this. But that still doesn't explain why he should want to buy something for me."

"I think it is obvious, Gwenda," Miss Thorne says, "he enjoys giving presents." She changes the subject.

"Now, have you written up your diary?"

"Not yet," Gwenda says, "I'm going to in a minute."

"That's good, but don't be too late to bed, deah. I'll say 'good night' then. *Morgen ist auch ein Tag*, Tomorrow is also a day."

"Miss Thorne."

"Yes?"

"Miss Thorne," Gwenda is shy. "I think Mr Frome is a bit like Wagner, don't you?"

Miss Thorne smiles. She closes the door behind her and crosses the room.

"Ah! Gwenda. So you think Mr Frome is like Wagner. In what way is Mr Frome like Wagner? Tell me, Gwenda, about Mr Frome and about Wagner."

Mrs Peabody feeling cold in the morning called her daughter back upstairs just as she was leaving.

"Dotty! I feel so cold. I feel so cold!"

"I'll miss my train mother! Mother, I'll be late and miss my train." Miss Peabody put her raincoat and her handbag on the hall chair and made a hot water bottle for her mother. She ran next door and asked Mrs Brewer to come in and look at her mother. The coldness of her hands and feet did not seem natural on a summer morning. In every other way her mother seemed perfectly well.

"Do you have a pain mother?" Miss Peabody asked. She tucked the bed covers in firmly.

"I'm all right Dotty. Nadine will sit with me for a little while. Off you go, you'll get the next train if you run." Mrs Brewer, who was in her plaid dressing gown and a knitted cap like a tea cosy, said,

"Yes you run along Dorothy. I'll 'phone the doctor if she doesn't warm up."

Mrs Peabody stopped living quickly, in about a quarter of an hour. She was dead before the doctor arrived. All he had to do, Mrs Brewer said, was to examine her and write out a death certificate.

"She died like a lady. Very quiet and dignified. A beautiful lady your mother, a real lady," Miss Peabody, who had come straight back from the office, thought she heard a note of accusation in Mrs Brewer's voice. The two women stood facing each other in the strangely empty bedroom. They were, after all the years of knowing each other, like strangers being together for no real reason.

"Well, I'd best be running along," Mrs Brewer said. She would have liked to disapprove openly of Dorothy's dry eyes. Being frequently acquainted with death during her life she knew that people often waited till they were alone before they broke down and wept. She could listen for Dorothy's grief from the staircase in her own house. "I'd best be running along," she said again.

"Yes, yes, I know you're busy," Miss Peabody said. "Thank you for all you've done for mother."

"Oh it was nothing," Mrs Brewer said.

For both of them, for the time being at least, their very reason for existence seemed to have been taken away.

In the evening Miss Peabody was able to sit down early to write to Diana and to tell her of the sudden death of her mother and how it was strange to remember that no one would be calling Dotty! Dotty! across the landing.

I am really ever so pleased to be able to write to you, Miss Peabody filled the page with the sudden death of Mrs Peabody. And I simply must thank you for the words from the Brahms Requiem. I have just been rereading them in your earlier letter. I am afraid you must think me very ignorant. I don't know the music at all. There is so much I don't know. I like the words, "How Lovely Is Thy Dwelling Place".

Miss Peabody thought of her mother somewhere in the most lovely pale blue surroundings. Rather like a clear summer day sky. There had been one such day this year. She pictured her mother gliding by on serene white clouds meeting old friends and even her husband, Miss Peabody's father. Perhaps as they glided they would think of her, look down on her and perhaps talk together about their daughter bravely going on with her daily life in spite of her bereavement. These thoughts were comforting.

Guiltily she pushed the novelist's letter into her drawer and went on to finish her own letter explaining that she was not sad over her mother's death.

What has to be has to be, she wrote, believing it and feeling that she had written something profound. She hoped Diana would not be too long in replying as she wanted to know more about Miss Thorne and the others in London. Please write soon about Miss Thorne and Miss Edgely. I am still trying to reason out, she wrote, how your writing can get me so emotionally involved. I feel I am having a disturbing experience.

She went to bed earlier than usual, tired with the day. As she feel asleep she hoped there would be a letter soon from the novelist.

Very sorry about your ma's death. It comes to us all — our own death that is, Diana's letter came so quickly, Miss Peabody realized she must have replied as soon as hers was received. You will notice, the novelist went straight on with other matters, you will notice that I am writing the story of Miss Thorne in the present tense. This makes it all very immediate. There are bound to be some people who will dislike this. One man's meat is another man's poison or some such stupid remark comes to my mind, you will know what I mean. If you feel disturbed and strange this is all perfectly natural. It is disturbing to explore the breast of a sixty year old woman in relation to a girl of sixteen. If you feel emotionally involved that is natural too. The writing is packed, it is dense writing, emotions on several levels packed in. It is, I hope, a novel of existence and feeling. A reader can be as involved as he wishes and some readers will fight off this involvement. Don't worry. Read on.

"So you like nice clothes Gwenda?" the novelist's ink was black and fresh and the words raced over the page.

"So you like nice clothes Gwenda? Gwenda! you cannot possibly accept such an expensive gift from a stranger. It must go back!" Miss Thorne, after breakfast, is in Gwenda's room. A sleepless night with Miss Edgely who disturbed the entire hotel at midnight looking for Miss Thorne when she was still with Gwenda, and the news at breakfast, from Gwenda, that a big, gift-wrapped box was delivered to her room first thing that morning causes Miss Thorne to enter Gwenda's little room without her customary knock and gentle question,

"May I come in Gwenda?"

Miss Thorne's nose is red. Miss Edgely has retired to drink hot water; it is one of her little customs on holiday. Miss Thorne, intending to order hot water for herself, has forgotten it for the time being. Her mind is on other things.

"But Miss Thorne I want to keep it! I've never had anything like this before." Gwenda, posing in front of the wardrobe mirror, turns to her Headmistress. "Isn't it lovely, Miss Thorne," she looks at herself again and turns her head to look at her back. "Isn't it lovely! I never thought a dress could feel so lovely. I don't feel a bit big or awkward in it. I've never felt like this before . . . "

"Gwenda! I am saying to you that it is not *comme il faut* to accept expensive presents from strangers."

"But Miss Thorne! You said yesterday I should have chosen a dress instead of . . . Please don't make me send it back. Please Miss Thorne. Please. I want to keep it. Please."

Miss Thorne steadies herself on the door as she closes it behind her. She is quite overcome by Gwenda's appearance. The girl baffles her. There is no question that Mr Frome knows exactly what is right for Gwenda to wear. As he said, he made a point of knowing what he needed to know. But this has nothing to do with Mr Frome getting his bread and butter. The effect here is something quite different. Gwenda is, by the cut of the cloth and by the blending of colour, transformed from a clumsy, pleasant schoolgirl into an attractive young woman. Furthermore her appearance gives the impression that she, to use a phrase which could be Mr Frome's, knows her own mind.

Gwenda turns slowly in front of the mirror looking over her shoulder again at the reflection of the back of the dress. The suggestion of silver and the vertical stripes do give a pleasing elegance. She turns again to Miss Thorne.

"Isn't it absolutely heavenly! It's a dream of a dress, Miss Thorne," Gwenda is radiant, "I've never had anything like this before. It's something my father could never afford for me now . . . "

"That's just it Gwenda," Miss Thorne is unable to bear the sight of this sophistication in the schoolgirl. "The dress must go straight back. You say yourself your father could not afford to give you a dress like that. I am reminding you that a young gel does not accept intimate presents from a strange man who is old enough to be her father. You will take orf the dress!"

"But he's not strange!" Gwenda's voice prevents Miss Thorne from leaving the room as she had intended after the command. "But he's not strange, Miss Thorne, he's Debbie's father, and you said last night he liked giving presents . . . I won't take it off! I want to wear it. Please Miss Thorne, I want to wear it."

"Gwenda," Miss Thorne interrupts, "I will leave you for half an hour to write up your diary. There is the Oscar Wilde play, *The Importance of Being Earnest* and the fashion parade, remember? And one more thing," Miss Thorne steps forward regarding the girl with narrowed eyes, "If you have no intention of returning the dress with a polite note of refusal; if you are going to insist on accepting it and wearing it, you will have to remember to stand well and to hold in your stomach."

Miss Thorne has hardly had the first sips of her hot water. She has put on her dressing gown and has taken out her notes on *Othello* to lift her mind from the Frome disturbance. She has feelings which she does not like to admit to herself. They are an echo, an unwanted echo, a refrain almost of Gwenda's whispered confidences during the night, "I do like Debbie's father, Miss Thorne don't you? When he talks to me I feel all warm and special, I feel I even look nice." *I feel I even look nice*, Miss Thorne knows this feeling too. She allows herself to dwell on it for a moment, before turning the next page of *Othello*.

It is one thing to have money to scatter on fees and on extras, speech training, languages, music, dancing, drama and travel but expensive gifts to schoolgirls are worrying. She wonders whether that young wife of Mr Manners, Rackette, or whatever her name was, had received so many gifts that there was nothing left over for Gwenda's needs. She wonders if all widowed fathers now, instead of respectably marrying their comfortable housekeepers, are given to eccentricities and indiscretions. She snorts.

"Too hot?" Miss Edgely asks. "The water? Is it too hot?"

"No deah, I was just thinking of middle-aged men."

"I thought you were doing *Othello*."

"Yes I am deah. Pass over that other jug will you."

There is no need to wonder, she tells herself, she knows all there is to know about parents of all kinds. It is clear that Gwenda is about to be or has been finally deserted by her parent. Miss Thorne has seen this before, many times. She remembers, in particular, a girl, Joan, whatever was her second name, no need for the name, Miss Thorne will never forget the face, the red eyes and red blotched cheeks and nose, the result of endless crying. The story was quite simple. The girl's mother ran off with an actor and the girl became deeply attached to her father. Holidays were spent with the father, the girl (like Gwenda later) becoming more and more devoted to him. Then suddenly he appears at school bringing with him a pretty young bride. They have come to say "Good bye" to Joan.

Miss Thorne, deciding then to keep Joan as a personal maid to the Headmistress, made one of the many mistakes she was to make during her time at the helm. She feels uncomfortable, even now all these years later, when she remembers how Joan tried to be both maid and schoolgirl as Miss Thorne hoped she would be.

The other girls decided, at that time, that maids were not students in a school like Pine Heights. Joan Lorne, Lorne — that was her other name — had been ostracized, there was no other name for it. Miss Thorne, overwhelmed just then with her discovery of Edgely, was busy coaxing secret feelings to the surface and did not pay sufficient attention to the responsibility she had so light-heartedly undertaken. Consequently the girl suffered insults upon insults, tricks and poor feeding, and, Miss Thorne feels even more ashamed when she thinks of it, no money. The girl had not the necessary self respect which belongs with having a little money in the pocket because Miss Thorne made it clear, though she gave her "her keep" of sorts, that she had no money to give her. Simply, from time to time a garment perhaps, something cast off. In the end the girl had become

118

ill in an unheated, unventilated room in the attic and had to be taken away.

Miss Thorne groans.

"More hot water?" Miss Edgely asks.

There is a knock at their door and a message to say a young lady and a gentleman are waiting to see Miss Thorne downstairs in the lounge.

Mr Frome and Debbie have come with an invitation to Gwenda to go for a drive in the afternoon, perhaps to Richmond or to Windsor.

"I'm afraid that's impossible, Mr Frome," Miss Thorne says. She remains standing so Mr Frome is not able to sit in one of the empty armchairs. "Thank you all the same," Miss Thorne says, "but this afternoon Gwenda, accompanied by Miss Edgely and myself, will be going to the theatre."

"Oh that's nice," Mr Frome says. "What's the play? I like a good play meself."

"It is part of the Oscar Wilde revival. Today is *An Ideal Husband*."

"Oh!" says Debbie, "that sounds good. What's it about? I mean what's the story line?"

"Rather difficult to put in a nutshell Debbie," Miss Thorne says in her kinder voice, "so much of Wilde depends on the way in which he says it . . . "

"Title's good enough for me," Mr Frome says. "*An Ideal Husband* eh? That sounds all right. I like the idea of that! Ideal husband eh?" he laughs. "Mind if we join you? I mean, we can have a drive any old time."

Debbie laughs.

"Oh dad! You are a one!" she turns to Miss Thorne, her eyes bright through her fringe, "Dad always goes to sleep at the pictures anyway!"

Miss Thorne smiles outwardly. How can the gel, she thinks to herself, after a whole term at Pine Heights not know the difference between a film and a stage play. Miss Thorne directs her continuing smile towards Mr Frome.

After all, even if he is impossibly common, he is clean and there is something pleasant about him. The possession of money, she considers this aspect, goes a long way towards making a man pleasant.

"I should be delighted," she says, "if you and Debbie would be able to accompany us. The afternoon performances are not at all crowded. I am sure we shall all be able to sit together. Debbie, you will benefit a great deal by seeing the play. It will be useful for your studies."

"That's all settled then," Mr Frome says, "we'll be there."

"Now, if you'll excuse me," Miss Thorne says, "I have something I must do."

"Well of course," Mr Frome says, "there's just one thing. Debbie here would like to run up and 'ave a word with Gwenda for a minute."

"Actually, Gwenda is busy just now with some school work," Miss Thorne is reluctant but forces herself to continue to be charming, "I'll show you which room is hers. I daresay she will spare you a few minutes."

"Thank you Miss Thorne."

"Much obliged," Mr Frome sits down opening his newspaper. "Off you go our Deb. I'll sit here luv and 'ave a read while you run upstairs. There's no 'urry. Take your time."

Miss Thorne is hardly back in her room with Miss Edgely when there is a soft little knock at the door.

"Yes? Come in!"

"Please Miss Thorne", the two girls are breathless in the doorway. They seem excited.

"Yes, what is it?"

"Please Miss Thorne, dad was wonderin' if it would be all right for Gwenda to come out t' shops for a little while. We'll not be long . . . "

"Have you lorst your tongue Gwenda?"

"No Miss Thorne. I'm sorry Miss Thorne." Gwenda smiles

at her Headmistress, "I would like to go and buy, I mean, Mr Frome thinks . . . "

"And exactly what does Mr Frome think?" Miss Thorne puts on her playful expression, peering at the girls in mock severity over her reading glasses.

"Well our dad thinks Gwenda should have some stockings for that dress."

"Gwenda?"

"Yes, Miss Thorne, Mr Frome thinks that the dress, that I need, that I should have . . . "

"Yes Gwenda?"

"They're called 'Cobweb Mist'," Debbie says, "they're lovely pantyhose, reelly thin and ever such a pale grey. Dad says they're the ones for the dress. They're lovely, I've got some, like they're made by spiders."

The girls shriek at the word "spiders" and clutch each other.

Miss Thorne laughs, "orf you go then, but don't be long. Remember Gwenda, we are supposed to be doing the British Museum this morning and we're having an early luncheon because of the play."

"Yes, Miss Thorne."

"You may go."

"Thank you Miss Thorne."

The emptiness Miss Thorne feels is alarming. She feels she should not feel it. Sitting in the cushionless cane chair in the hotel bedroom, she tries to read and to make notes.

An hour goes by and Gwenda does not return. Miss Thorne tries to read something about Wagner and discovers with horror that, unless she is talking to Gwenda about Wagner, she does not have any real interest.

She finds herself thinking of Mr Frome. In his own way, though she does not like to admit it, she has to acknowledge that there is something very natural and nice about him. He is almost attractive and he almost certainly finds her attractive. Miss Thorne knows she would like to cultivate something in Mr Frome. Perhaps at the theatre during the interval when the tea is brought in, the girls could be sent off for an ice, and she would have the chance to chat with Mr Frome. Perhaps a few words first about Debbie's successful progress at school, perhaps a little about the play, Mr Frome might well need some help with that, and then, to make the most of the chance, to talk to him about the school. The thought of Miss Edgely, who will be there too, irritates her. Edgely can't be sent off for an ice. It is a nuisance that Edgely is present. At the back of her mind now, something not quite nice, is nagging. She must read. She opens her *Othello* at the place where she made notes for production.

But jealous souls will not be answered so:
They are not ever jealous for the cause,
But jealous for they are jealous . . .

She looks at her watch, nearly two hours. She is not used to wasting a morning. She feels restless and annoyed,

"We'll never get to the museum now." Miss Edgely tries to look sympathetic. She is enjoying the comfortable morning with a *True Story* magazine. "It's always a shame to miss the museum, don't you think? To forego the treasures of Acadeemia!" Miss Thorne, ignoring Miss Edgely, gets up suddenly from her bony chair.

"I'll just go and see if Gwen — if the gel's back. She may have come in and gorn straight to her room." Miss Thorne taps at the door of Gwenda's little room.

"May I come in Gwenda?" There is no answer. She opens the door. The room is empty and, as usual, very tidy, except that the new dress is spread out on the bed. Gwenda's writing things are on the dressing table. Miss Thorne pulls open the top drawer and, with competent hands, in spite of herself, pulls forth Gwenda's diary. The pages are neatly and firmly written in the familiar Pine Heights handwriting. Miss Thorne does not read them but flips through them, letting them slip over one after the other. She smiles to herself with approval and with the satisfaction of knowing that her enthusiastic instruction, during the holiday, has not been wasted. The last page is only half covered and there is an entry in another hand; possibly Debbie has been invited to contribute something this morning. Miss Thorne smiles at the thought of Gwenda showing Debbie her diary. What could be a better way of starting a deep friendship.

The writing is even and sloping and ornamental. It is someone's best writing; there are little flourishes and a correction or two. Miss Thorne, unable to resist, reads the curly loops.

Miss Thorne blinks. She is unable to understand what is written there. Something about Future Wife and Helen of Troy and Bedroom. She has no idea who can have written the sentence. Who can have entered Gwenda's room and written in her diary? Certainly it is very suggestive and is written by an uneducated person, but Debbie would not have written about a future wife. Miss Thorne ponders on the mixed images. She smiles over the Helen of Troy,

"Hyperbole! Hyperbole! The perfect example," she says to herself.

Under the heading of *The Importance of Being Earnest* where Gwenda has obviously been meaning to write her comments on the play, someone, the same person judging by the handwriting, has drawn a bent arrow to the *Earnest* and the words, *I like that*, are written underneath; a little line of correction crosses out the *a* in *Earnest*. She smiles again about the Helen of Troy. "An unimaginative attempt at the expression of beauty," she mutters to herself, "I am entirely unable to understand your notion of capital letters and punctuation," she says aloud and replaces the diary under the neatly folded blouses and pantyhose.

* * *

Miss Peabody knew that she would recognize them when she saw them. Gwenda always wore her school blazer and her school hat; the novelist had mentioned this. Now that she, Gwenda, had the new dress she might want to leave off the blazer. Miss Peabody felt certain that Miss Thorne would never allow this; she was sure to insist that Gwenda must be neatly dressed in school uniform.

All three travellers would be easily recognizable. Gwenda's blazer was light blue. Miss Thorne would wear the dark blue denim suit with the white blouse and Miss Edgely, her scarcely worn polyester trouser suit.

The Oscar Wilde plays would be in one of the older theatres. Miss Peabody wished she knew which one so that she could wait near by and see them arrive or leave.

Diana had been vague about which hotel. There was a reference to "a not so good part of London". Miss Peabody was nervous to walk alone in back streets especially now when so many people were unemployed and dangerously discontented. There were a lot of coloured people about too. The subject often came up at the Fortress Friday parties. Mr Bains had strong views on the problem.

"You can call them West Indians but they are negroes you know, they are negroes. If they're deprived it's their own fault . . . "

"Where is *An Ideal Husband*?" Miss Peabody piped bravely in the Wild West Ranch Room. With two brandies down and one in the hand she planted herself in front of Mr Bains.

"Where is *An Ideal Husband*?" Miss Peabody asked again, straddling her steel legs and turning up her crooked chin to make her cheeky expression. Mr Bains was clearly embarrassed. He felt he was being criticized. A vision of Mrs Bains, Margaret, always waiting, restless on committees, madly joining in tennis and Bridge, but always waiting, lonely with their two sad-eyed children, floated before him.

"She's drunk!" Mr Bains muttered to Miss Truscott.

"Oh Lord! Not again!" Miss Truscott slipped off her high stool showing shapely gun-metal thighs.

"Would you like to lie down, dear?"

Miss Peabody noticed, with approval, Miss Truscott's legs. She thought she would like to display her own. She tried to grab a stool.

"No dear, you can't lie on a stool." Miss Truscott guided Miss Peabody through the crowd to the Ladies where she, more or less, threw her on the chaise longue.

"There dear!" she said with fierce lips. "Stay! Till you are better enough to go home." She was sorry about the sudden death of Miss Peabody's mother. All the office were sorry, but what could anyone do?

" 'I'm a little prairie flower'," sang Miss Peabody. Miss Truscott flushed the toilet and fled.

"There's only the two of them and the girl," Miss Peabody did not lie down for long. She thought she would walk out into the warmth of the long afternoon. She would look for the theatre. Mr Frome and Debbie might be with them. It would not be hard to know them, unless they had gone for their drive after all. With mother gone there was absolutely no need to hurry home.

She felt annoyed with herself for not being cultured enough to know what was on and where in London. *Sound of Music*? *Dr Zhivago*? she thought, but they were years ago. A Gold Exhibition? Oh, years ago too. She thought she would buy a paper and look up the entertainments. This intelligent idea gave her pleasure.

"Excuse me!" Miss Peabody stopped a woman on the pavement. "I've come without my reading glasses, could you just read for me please?" She handed the folded page of newspaper, "I'm looking for *An Ideal Husband*."

"Aren't we all, ducks! Best of luck to you! I've just walked out on mine. Good luck! I'm in a hurry! If you'll excuse me."

Miss Peabody tried again. This time a man,

"Six kids," he said, "Sorry, I'm terribly married. Six kids. Good night."

"Everyone's in such a hurry," Miss Peabody complained. She walked a considerable distance crazily looking up at the sky. It occurred to her that it was possible that some path of sky between the high buildings would broaden out into a kind of harbour. That would be the place where Miss Thorne and Miss Edgely would be with Gwenda trailing along; all needing a friend in London.

"I always feel dazed myself when I come out of a matinee," Miss Peabody practised her most sympathetic voice in readiness. She would, she thought, take them for afternoon tea. There was sure to be a place open still. She wished she had studied the hours of tea shops more carefully.

"Hey! Take more water with it!"

"Watch my corns willya! I don't grow 'em to be tramped on."

"Lady! Look where you're goin'. Buses kill."

"An Ideal Husband eh? Take it from me, there's no such thing."

"I always feel a bit guilty myself going to a matinee," Miss Peabody said in a voice charged with understanding, "it's like time out, in a sense, you know, a bit daring and depraved, I mean, to go out in the afternoons on pleasure bent."

"Watch your state Missis," a voice said. Someone tugged her skirt down into place.

"I'm Miss, not Missis. Could you tell me where *An Ideal Husband* is?" Miss Peabody seemed to see the towers and spires and the high buildings as if they were upside down and under her feet. The grass smelled sweet crushed so near her face.

"I love this park," she said, "I really love this park. Always have loved this park. Park I say every day I love you."

"That's right," the man's kind voice said, "just you lie down till you feel better."

Miss Peabody saw all the buildings jump and roll as she felt herself tilted back. She felt herself being covered over with something.

" 'When the church came to itself . . . ' " she said, " 'I was seated on a high tombstone' — that's Dickens," she said. She laughed. "Have you read Pip?" she asked. "You know Pip in the marshes when the convict picks him up — it's literally years and years since I read that book."

It was a misfortune for Mr Bains that Miss Peabody chose his name and his home telephone number as someone the police could call upon. He drove all the way from Surrey to rescue her.

The message came at six in the morning. Unwillingly, propped on one elbow, eyes squinting, he listened to the details.

"I'll come right over," he said, trying not to be disagreeable into the telephone.

He had, making an excuse to Pam Truscott the night before, made up his mind to spend the whole of Saturday and Sunday with Margaret and the children. Strangers. Margaret, his children, they were more like strangers. What was he to them, he asked himself. Family life needs preserving in this unsettled day and age he insisted in his head. After the Fortress party, depositing the indignant and pouting Truscott on her own clean doormat, with the mulberry overnight bag placed quickly beside her, he drove straight home. Taking his wife by surprise on the stairs, he had rushed her, with mounting passion, up into the bedroom.

"What's the matter Dear? What time is it?" Margaret Bains raised her sleep-heavy hair net from the pillow.

"Oh it's nothing. Nothing at all. Go back to sleep. I'll have to go up to town. One of our clerical staff in some kind of mild trouble. I'll have to sort it out."

* * *

Miss Peabody, assisted by Mr Bains, entered her house by way of the drain pipe. It enabled her to clamber on to the coal house roof. From there it was possible to crawl through the bathroom window. This window, which was very small, was always open.

It was not easy for Mr Bains. The house was completely locked; naturally it was locked in order to keep people out.

"It must have fallen out of my bag," Miss Peabody giggled, "when I was upside down in the park." She was quite unable to find her key, searching her pockets and her handbag. "Oh I do feel ever so awful Mr Bains," she said. "Really I feel terrible to be such a nuisance."

Mr Bains was only just able to restrain himself from shaking her. Dishevelled and unwashed, Miss Peabody was not a pretty sight. Mr Bains looked away. It was awkward to be standing there in the front garden early on a Saturday morning. Anyone in the street could see them, and it would be obvious they were trying to get into the house. He could not stand carelessness or stupidity and now confronted with both and without breakfast he said,

"I don't think I can get through that window, but if you can, I can give you a lift up the pipe."

"Oh yes, I've been in that way before, but not for many years." Miss Peabody blinked up at him through her crooked glasses. "Thank you so much."

It was quite without magic being underneath Miss Peabody. She was much heavier than he had imagined.

"Heave Ho!" Miss Peabody cried, her heel caught his forehead, a sharp cutting blow. The blood flowed. Miss Peabody did not notice.

"Father always told me never to look down," she called.

Mr Bains did not watch the last part. He turned away a second time. From the corner of his eye, however, he was aware of her two legs in "steel" waving frantically as she worked her way into the small space of the window. He supposed, knowing the general pattern of bathrooms in such houses, she would land in the bath.

He went round to the front of the house expecting Miss Peabody to open the front door from inside. He waited a considerable time and then knocked at the door and, after a few minutes, rang the bell. There was the sound of a muffled voice,

"Just a minute," the front door opened a fraction.

"Not today, thank you," Miss Peabody snapped and closed the door.

Mr Bains waited.

"She can't still be tight!" he said to himself as he heard muffled shrieks from inside the house.

"I'm a little prairie flower," he heard her singing, *"Growing wilder every hour."*

"If she's not tight," he said to himself, "she's mad."

Mr Bains left.

In the evening Miss Peabody wrote to Diana. Did they, Miss Thorne and the others, ever get to the play, she wanted to know. Are Miss Thorne and Mr Frome going to get married? I love happy endings, she wrote. Men, she wrote, often appeared to be attracted to someone but really are only using that person to get to someone else. There was a girl called Audrey in my class at school, she told the novelist, I used to have to pass notes from her to a boy. I liked this boy and he seemed to like me, I mean, he spoke to me, but all the time he was reaching out to that Audrey. Of course I only realized this much later. Mr Frome, Miss Peabody wrote, might appear to look at Gwenda but he would naturally choose an older, more mature woman.

Miss Peabody gasped, she put down her pen. Miss Edgely, of course, the little prairie flower in the shadow of the thorn bush. How it all fitted together! Mr Frome was obviously fond of Miss Edgely, one only had to remember that meal when he poured brandy for her. Miss Peabody took up her pen again. Dear Diana, she wrote, please write soon I have been looking for them in London. You have not said where they are . . .

The reply came quickly.

Plato, the novelist wrote, says that the poet is a light and holy winged thing, and there is no invention in him until he is inspired out of his senses . . .

Miss Peabody, from habit, saved the letter till the evening. She liked the evenings to belong to the novelist.

Miss Thorne's plan for an early lunch before the theatre has not fallen through, excuse the cliché, the novelist wrote, I'll underline it in red as usual. They are all except for Edgely, who is late, sitting together, she wrote, lunch has been served. Mr Frome has come straight to the point.

"I'm a blunt man," he tells Miss Thorne. "I want to tell you something. I've asked Gwenda here to marry me and she's accepted."

Miss Thorne, who has ordered a poached egg on haddock, unwisely pricks the egg with her fork. She looks across at Mr Frome ignoring the egg yolk as it flows freely over the fish. The entry in the diary slips into place.

Whatever can Mr Frome know about Helen of Troy, Miss Thorne thinks, perhaps in trying to flatter and please the gel he chose an idea of beauty, well known and with popular appeal. She continues to regard Mr Frome steadily.

"I need a wife," he says, "it's as simple as that. I've been a widder all these years because I've never seen or met anyone to take our Deb's mother's place. Now," he smiles in the direction of the two girls, "Now I've met Gwenda. She's the one for me and what's more, though I can hardly believe it, she's said 'yes'."

"But this is ludicrous Mr Frome!" Miss Thorne says with her own way of being blunt. "The gel's still at school, she's only a school gel. She cannot possibly accept your proposal. She's only sixteen."

"Seventeen next month," Mr Frome says. "I've got a note of her birthday here so I don't forget to get her a nice card," he laughs and pats his pocket where his wallet is. "She's had enough schooling for me," he continues, "she's very nicely educated. You've done very good job w' the lass."

"I suppose you realize Gwenda has a father." Miss Thorne feels powerless and this makes anger begin to rise in her. "While her father is away, I have the responsibility, which I do not take lightly, of looking after Gwenda." Controlling her anger, Miss Thorne smiles with real affection at Gwenda who smiles at her Headmistress with shining eyes.

"Yes, I know Gwenda has a father," Mr Frome says, "we sent her dad a cable this morning to ask his permission."

"I see," Miss Thorne makes an effort to be agreeable. She will speak to Gwenda later. It is not the right time now.

Gwenda is sitting with her chair pulled very close to Mr Frome's. One of his crisp woollen arms slips round her back; he gives her a playful squeeze.

Miss Thorne cannot help reflecting that he must be over twenty years older than Gwenda. Not that age really matters, she is quite honest to herself. It is simply the fact that he is the father of another schoolgirl. He is Debbie Frome's father. The other consideration is the extraordinary, the amazing speed with which he has conducted his affairs. Miss Thorne ignores Gwenda's happy little wriggle beneath the magic arm.

"Well Debbie," Miss Thorne says with one of her more pleasant smiles, apparently ignoring her fork, useless in the egg. "What do you think about the proposed marriage?" Miss Thorne thinks tact is quite unnecessary. "Do you mind?"

"Mind?" Debbie peers at Miss Thorne through her long

131

fringe. "Mind? Why should I mind? Miss Thorne, why should I mind? I think it's great!" she grins. "I think Gwenda's just right for dad. If he's happy an' she's happy that's O.K. with me." Her eyes dart through the fringe. "She'll get dad off my back. That she will! And another thing, I've not seen dad happy like this before."

Miss Edgely, who is late for lunch, comes in and sits down to the cold ham salad Miss Thorne, to save time, had the sense to order for her.

Miss Thorne, allowing her mind to dwell on the possible and the impossible, wonders how Debbie Frome will feel at the time of the closing of the bedroom door. She blows her nose and cleans it with her usual vigour. The thought of the quiet click, the final click when the shared bedroom door is closed, is too much for her. No doubt for Debbie Frome the secret sound will be drowned in disco or worse. Miss Thorne hears that click now all too clearly.

Gwenda, looking across the table at her Headmistress smiles. It is not quite her usual smile. For Mr Frome and Debbie the meal is finished. The others, Pine Heights fashion, are moving little heaps of food about on their plates. Miss Thorne, as she adds something indefinite to the small, but growing, mound of spinach, is considering the arrangements she can make for sending Gwenda back to school that evening. Bales and Mrs Bales will have to come off board wages a few days earlier to look after her.

There would be a certain relief, she feels, to be alone in London, alone just with Miss Edgely, that is. Mr Frome's presence, his energy and his intention are making her tired. In any case his intention must be diverted. The object of his attention can easily be removed. She rises from the table. She will send a telegram immediately. Accustomed to thinking quickly, all kinds of thoughts pour through her head. She is disturbed by their disquieting nature. It is a pity, she thinks, that Mr Frome uncovered, at once, Miss Edgely's little weakness, which, though not the same beverage, is not so far from her own need. Though, Heaven forbid! her need is not in the same category as Edgely's. There is too that long list of idiotic Grinzings. When looked at from a distance they seem incredible; they are in fact all too credible and carry with them nothing creditable for the School. Miss Thorne bears all these thoughts. As she leaves the table she smiles across at both schoolgirls.

"If either of you gels have any letters or picture postcards written and ready for posting, I have some and am just about to walk down the street to the letter box. I will be pleased to take yours with mine. And, after that, we simply must leave to be in time for Oscar Wilde."

Miss Thorne knows that it only takes a minute to scribble a line of gossip. It only needs one girl to receive it and, in a few days, when the school is reassembled, rumour will become fact, fact will become history and, something Miss Thorne refuses to think of, prophecy. She is tempted to confine Gwenda to her own room for the whole afternoon while arrangements for her return to school are made.

This discipline, one of the more successful at Pine Heights, is hardly acceptable during a short holiday in London. How can it be said, when the tickets are bought and they are about to set off for the theatre, that Oscar Wilde is out of bounds. It is comforting, in this disturbing time, to think of the Pine Heights Discipline, the production of *Othello*, the orchestra practising the chosen Brandenburg Concerto, and the song writing competition for the creation of the new saint, Saint Pine. Miss Thorne is surprised to find herself actually wishing to see Mr Minsk. She thinks, with some longing, of the pine needly path and the fragrance of that little walk between the School House and her own apartment in the Boarding House. She thinks of the school paddock and the orchard with its meagre but prized fruit. And then there are the school gardens. Such neglect! Bales must be pulled sharply to heel! He must grow more vegetables. What could be healthier and cheaper than home grown cabbages.

Gwendaline Manners, Miss Thorne thinks, for her own sake needs discipline to rescue her from the absurd.

She thinks of the school and its safety with pleasure. The school is a kind of fortress.

Miss Peabody never told anyone at the office that her key was in her handbag all the time that day when Mr Bains helped her to break into her own house.

"Never was I so glad to see a friendly face," she made the most of the rescue story for some time explaining how she had been her own burglar, being careful never to mention the key which she found as soon as she was inside the house. She wrote several pages describing Mr Bains and his strength to the novelist and waited eagerly for a reply.

About two weeks later, Mr Bains, after a short interview with Miss Truscott, sent for Miss Peabody.

Mr Bains had put off seeing Miss Peabody. Now he felt he could not go on putting off the meeting. He had not enjoyed fetching her from the police station lock up. It was an embarrassment to be asked to identify someone he did not care to know. It was one thing to tolerate Miss Peabody in the office, making mistakes daily at a safe distance from him, but to be asked to go along like a relative, or worse, like a friend to fetch her from that disgusting place was quite different. Oh, the place had been clean enough but disgusting all the same. The reason for its existence disgusted him. Margaret would never . . . but why even think of Margaret in the same context. Not even Pam would have . . . Unthinkable!

He supposed, during that day, that he could have refused to do what he did. Somehow he felt he was responsible. Second in command in a large organization often had these minor responsibilities. On his way home that day after pushing Miss Peabody up the drain pipe he had driven by

Pam Truscott's flat. The curtains were drawn to the quiet street. No doubt she was still asleep. Poor Pam, she hung with such happiness on his arm whenever they were going off together. He hated having to disappoint her, to leave her alone. As he went by he almost stopped because the flat looked desolate in the block of lonely dwellings. He pulled into the kerb thinking he would go in and give her a surprise.

"Before or after brekky?" she would ask in that hoarse voice of hers. "Or both?" she would laugh, "let's make whoopee!" she would shriek. Pam, like Margaret, was predictable but not quite as boring. Both said the same things but Pam said hers with a kind of vulgarity which would have made Margaret blush.

He pulled out from the kerb. Margaret, she was alone too. She was alone too often at the weekends. Neighbours were sure to gossip. Barry Bains could not stand gossip. Resolutely driving away from Pam Truscott towards Margaret, perhaps because of Miss Peabody, he felt even more stifled. Tangled utterly in female arms and legs.

He held his head in both hands now resting his elbows on his polished desk, waiting for Miss Peabody. He had hated having to admit, in public, acquaintance with her and he had hated even more having to drive the silly woman home listening to her grasshopper chatter on what she called topical subjects.

"Miss Peabody. There you are! Please sit down." Mr Bains jumped up to place a chair for Miss Peabody as she sidled through the door towards him.

"Cigarette?"

"Oh thank you, I don't mind if I do."

"Miss Peabody," Mr Bains said, "we, those of us in charge here at Fortress, feel you need, I mean, deserve, yes deserve, a long holiday. I am suggesting that you take three months off and er, your er, position will be reviewed after that."

"Oh thank you Mr Barrington."

"Bains."

"Oh yes, of course, it's Mr Bains. Thank you. I have been feeling very tired. It's the excitement, I mean it's mother's death. It was so sudden . . ."

"Yes. Yes," he murmured. "Tired. Yes," he made his own tired face as kindly as he could. He thought he might be dead before Miss Peabody reappeared. The possibility cheered him. He smiled. Placing his finger tips together he said,

"Have you somewhere? Have you some place in mind where you would like to go? For a complete rest and a change? I mean, people do need a change from time to time," he paused and then went on quickly, "and we at Fortress are prepared to help you financially. I, er, wondered if somewhere on the south coast perhaps?"

"Oh No! That will not be necessary," Miss Peabody said, "I have Blood Pressure," she added.

"Yes. Yes, we all have. Indeed we all have." Mr Bains did not try to understand where blood pressure fitted in with railway fares.

"I'll go to Australia," Miss Peabody said. "I have a friend there. She is a Goddess you know. Diana. Artemis. Folk Goddess of the Grecians. Daughter of Zeus. Diana. The Lord of Free Nature. She goes hunting on the mountains with her maidens. She is the sister of Apollo. She is," Miss Peabody paused, "She is also the Goddess of the Moon."

Mr Bains crept to the door and beckoned to Miss Truscott.

"Take her away!" he managed to whisper, mouthing the words so that Miss Truscott would understand what he was saying without anyone hearing his voice.

"Take her away!"

So much depends, the novelist wrote, her reply coming quickly after Miss Peabody's description of her adventures with Mr Bains, so much depends in the writing of a novel on the impact of the imagination on someone else. A great deal depends too on the fiction which is mounted on truth. Take landscape, for example: forests are more mysterious, paddocks are lengthened and widened, escarpments are pushed to greater heights and brought closer to townships. The writer creates the imagined land from fragments of the real thing . . .

Of course, in the letter, there was no mention of Miss Peabody's visit because Miss Peabody, thinking to surprise Diana, had not written about her intention to travel. She sat at her dressing table, as usual, to read Diana's letter which was written in the flamboyant violet ink badly smudged in places.

"You don't know your own strength Ella," Miss Edgely, purple faced after a vigorous shaking, manages to say. "It's all very well for you, Ella, you've got everything going for you. You're a sort of Goddess. You can hunt for whatever you want and take it. Don't think I didn't notice you at the theatre with that man. I wasn't asleep as you thought. I saw you send the girls off for ice cream and I saw you, with my own eyes, making up to that man. Ella how could you! I mean Ella how could you! I suppose you're going to marry him. Did he ask you, Ella, to marry him? Did he?" Miss Edgely, still a bit discoloured after Miss Thorne's treatment, bursts into tears. "Oh Ella!" she sobs.

"But Edge! There was nothing. There is nothing I assure you!" Miss Thorne, her anger spent after the good shaking she has given Miss Edgely, is full of remorse. She remembers too that Edgely was late for luncheon. She came down to the meal after Mr Frome's announcement.

"Oh Edge do stop that noise! You are quite mistaken in what you think you saw. Naturally I made a little polite conversation with Mr Frome, I mean, with that man. He does not interest me at all. Now will you please be quiet. I'm thinking," Miss Thorne closes her eyes.

Miss Edgely is quiet for a few moments.

"By the way," she asks brightly, "what did you think of the play? I often wonder what the Academic litterati think of Oscar Wilde. I mean he wasn't quite normal was he . . . "

"Oh Pax Edge! Please! I'm thinking. I simply don't know what you mean. Who are the Academic litterati, for Heaven's Sake! What a ghastly phrase!"

Miss Edgely starts to cry again, shuddering as she draws tragic breath.

Miss Edgely's way of stopping Miss Thorne from doing what she wants to do is infuriating. Miss Thorne is trying to compose something in her head to say or write to Gwenda warning her of the unsatisfactory nature and the danger of a relationship with an older man. She wants to tell Gwenda that she will, later on, meet a young man with skin as clear and fresh as her own, a young man to match her in youth and in passionate love. She wants to tell her that she will have all she is wishing for. She will have her little alpine plot. She remembers the quotation from Goethe,

And she on the torrent's edge in childish simplicity
In a little hut in a little alpine field,
And all her household things
Gathered in that small world.

She wants to tell Gwenda that this is all ahead of her with someone else, that she does not need to fall into the arms of the first man who says a kind word to her. While she is thinking, with considerable heartache, of Gwenda's soft, youthful, fresh body and her smile of real pleasure at having Miss Thorne as a special friend, Miss Edgely is fussing and crying and being a nuisance.

Miss Thorne is on the point of a decision to leave London the following day. All three of them to pack up and leave to go home by the quickest route. There is really no alternative. She has failed in her intention to send Gwenda back.

After the play Mr Frome simply said that he was taking the girls out for the evening. They were to hurry and get changed into their new dresses, he said.

"I'd like to take them to a slap-up place for a bit of posh dinner. There's no need to wait up for Gwenda," he told Miss Thorne, "We might do a late night show. See?" he said. "I'll see young Gwenda safely back, there's nought to worry about! She's safe with me."

The loss of Gwenda and Miss Edgely's constant crying and nagging nearly leads to further violence. Miss Thorne, controlling herself, tries to stop thinking about Gwenda.

"Come on Edge old gel," she consoles. "Come on Edge!" she says in a low voice. "Take a hot bath. Don't cry any more. Look! I've said I'm sorry. Let's both have a nice hot bath. All this emotion has made us a bit whiffy you know. Come on, Edge, race you to the bath!"

The night is warm, Miss Thorne pours a substantial brandy for Miss Edgely and lines up a little fortification of double whiskies, in prudent containers, on the bedside table.

" 'Come away to bed swee-sweedle,' " Miss Thorne decides it is too warm a night for nightdresses.

"I'm absooty bonkers over you Edge deah! No more silliness and crying eh? Eh? Sweedle?" Miss Thorne holds out both arms.

"Come away to bed . . . "

"Come in!" Miss Thorne, half asleep, raises her head as she hears the little knock on the door. "Come in!" she calls before she is fully awake. She hears Gwenda's soft voice.

"I'm back Miss Thorne."

Miss Thorne, trying to pull the counterpane quickly over her own and Miss Edgely's sleeping nakedness, sees the startled look on the girl's face as she draws back immediately from the remarkable scene.

"Good night Miss Thorne." The door closes quickly with a firm little click. Miss Thorne hears this final click with more pain than relief. She feels angry as she tucks the bed clothes round the unlovely, sleeping Miss Edgely. She forgets that this evening she has remembered and known again the cool softness of Edgely's lips. She forgets too the large tears which welled and trembled along Edgely's eyelashes.

She sits in the cushionless chair by the partly open window listening to the summer night sounds. There is a quality of delicate tenderness in the unexpected, sweet fragrance of grass, perhaps cut that day. Possibly there is a tiny lawn somewhere below, tucked in beside the steps which are between the front door and the street. The hotel and the district are squalid, representing the lonely side of human life. Miss Thorne does not even wince at the cliché in her own mind. The sudden fragrance, because of the endless pavements and ugly streets, is the more special. Miss Thorne likes the idea of a carefully looked after patch of grass in those surroundings. She thinks of the sweet curve of Gwenda's neck and of her rather thick but smooth girlish shoulders. And she thinks of her hopeful white breasts. Gwenda is so innocent and has such innocent secret wishes. Miss Thorne wants to speak to her to somehow remove from the girl's mind the horrible sight, as it must have been to her, when she opened the door.

The room, Miss Thorne thinks, has no space for anything, not even for perversion if it must be called that. Bodies in passion need to toss themselves and to be tossed. Where could anyone stretch out or reach out in love and in passion in such a narrow room and on such a narrow bed. She does not look at the disfigured bed. It simply is not profitable to spend time wondering why hotels invest in cheap frail furniture. The idea that there is something ridiculous in a travelling Headmistress and her entourage leaving behind them a trail of broken beds does not present itself to her.

Why ever, Miss Thorne thinks with anger at herself, why ever did they leave the light on and why ever did they neglect to lock their door. Naturally, seeing the light through the fanlight over the door, Gwenda knocked to report that she had returned and to say "Good night". She was simply being the product of her Pine Heights upbringing. Miss Thorne sits on in the uncomfortable chair.

Perhaps the gel could understand, she thinks to herself, perhaps the gel could understand something of the real need people have in themselves, a need matching needs in other people. If she chose her words and phrases carefully, perhaps she could tell Gwenda about Edgely's little scent bottle, Ashes of Roses it was called; Miss Thorne remembers how touched she was years ago when she discovered this childish possession. It would be a way of explaining to Gwenda if she could speak to her about Miss Edgely's Ashes of Roses. After all, there are the times that she has spent alone with Gwenda. Miss Thorne wonders if Gwenda will remember them as clearly as she, Miss Thorne, will, with tenderness, remember and cherish them.

It is a nuisance about that man, Mr Frome. As the hours go by Miss Thorne feels certain that, once back at school, Gwenda will forget all about him and simply look back on him as a stocky little man, rich of course, but entirely unimportant. He will become once more simply the father of one of the schoolgirls.

It is possible, Miss Thorne reasons, working her way to the last glass of Scotch, that Gwenda is still awake. She is probably excited and she might be upset. Miss Thorne feels it is her duty to slip on her dressing gown and go along the passage to Gwenda's little room and knock at the door saying,

"May I come in Gwenda?"

There is no answer to Miss Thorne's soft knock. She opens the door and quietly peers into the room. By the light of the street lamp outside she can see that the room is empty. She thinks she has made a mistake and is in the wrong room. She looks at the room number; it is the correct one. She switches on the light. It is clear that Gwenda has been to bed because the bed clothes are disturbed. She must have tried to go to sleep.

There is nothing of Gwenda's in the room, no clothes, no shoes or writing things, there were not many things but all that she had are gone.

Miss Thorne feels numb. She is afraid. On the corner of the dressing table is an envelope addressed to her in the familiar handwriting. It is so like Gwenda to be neat and thoughtful. The note is very brief, it simply says that Miss Thorne should not be worried; the note is meant for reading at breakfast time. There is a little explanation.

"I have packed my things and gone round to the Frome Hotel. Miss Thorne, I hope you will not mind but I would like to go with Debbie to visit her grandma." The next words and the letter's ending are all blurred because of the tears which fill Miss Thorne's sleepless eyes. Unaccustomed to crying she finds it hard to breathe. She puts the letter in her dressing gown pocket and stumbles back along the passage to the room she shares with Miss Edgely.

Miss Peabody, on her way to visit Diana, thought that being in a plane was like sitting inside an enormous flying cat. She could hear the happy purring as the cat flew through and above the masses of white cloud. She thought that this quiet calm feelng must be what it would be like after death. This was what heaven must be like.

It was the calmness of committing oneself and of being committed. It was, she told herself, a time of no return.

"It simply is not possible to get out, is it?" she said, with her brightest smile, to the passenger next to her. "I mean, I can't walk out there can I," she said.

As soon as he could the man in the adjoining seat asked the pretty air hostess if he could move.

"Twenty hours is twenty hours," he muttered with a sideways look at Miss Peabody.

From a quick glance at the last letter, received as she was leaving, Miss Peabody realized she was travelling not so far behind Miss Thorne who would, by now, be back at Pine Heights; perhaps even at this moment, carving the meat.

Miss Thorne and Miss Edgely lose each other in London, the novelist's familiar generous handwriting spread over the pages, a simple misunderstanding. Miss Edgely waits unsuccessfully for Miss Thorne on the wrong street corner for twelve hours. Miss Thorne, with some misgivings, having finished her last minute shopping, flies back alone. Pinned to the lapel of her denim jacket she has an orchid; she feels sure it is an orchid, sprayed with some sort of pink glitter. It was delivered to the breakfast table at the hotel accompanied by a pink scallopped card decorated with the ornamental signature of Ernest Frome. A little message of love written in Gwenda's careful round handwriting is finished off with the quick nimble name of Debbie Frome.

There was a flower for Miss Edgely too, a smaller one than Miss Thorne's. The difference in size being quite suitable, Miss Thorne thinks with approval. She, Miss Thorne, is both touched and relieved. The language of the flower sets her mind at rest, at least partly at rest.

Oh dear, the banal language, "the language of the flower", I shall put this in order in the rewriting, the novelist underlined the sentence with three heavy lines of red. Also "sets her mind at rest." Awful!

Miss Thorne, receiving the flower, understands that Gwenda will not, after her midnight flight to the Frome Hotel, have confided the ridiculous and shameful scene she had the misfortune to come upon.

An even more relieving, and perhaps at the same time perplexing, thing is that squeezed on the back of the card is the news that both girls will be three weeks late returning to school and that a cheque for fees is on the way. Also, will Miss Thorne consider selling her paddock to Mr Frome.

Miss Peabody quickly slipped the letter back into her new handbag and, imitating the other passengers, obediently ate the contents of the little white tray placed before her by the stewardess. She ate the crumbed sausage, the olive and the pineapple ring and, without shame, still copying the others, she inspected and then ate the fruit salad and ice cream. Unaccustomed, she almost ate the moist tissue. It was folded in blue and silver foil and looked attractive like an unusual sweet.

Miss Edgely would be returning all alone, she thought. Having missed Miss Thorne she would be on a later flight. Possibly she was somewhere on this one. Miss Peabody looked up with expectation every time anyone passed. Of course she knew she would not recognize Miss Edgely on her own, even if she was wearing the tartan polyester trouser suit. She would need to see them all together. Gwenda, in her school uniform, was essential. As individuals they were unrecognizable.

Meanwhile the long journey continued. Progress towards destination was inevitable. Travelling seemed serene, though there were uncertainties.

"I mean, people do get lost," Miss Peabody said to herself. "Yet," she said to the stewardess, "yet when Miss Edgely gets lost it does not seem to matter. She always gets back to Miss Thorne, or rather, Miss Thorne always finds Miss Edgely."

"That's good! Tea or coffee?" The hostess took the little white plastic tray.

"Tea please. Thank you." Miss Peabody drank her tea and thought it would be amusing to write once more to Diana Hopewell. Since the extraordinary correspondence started Miss Peabody found she had an overwhelming wish to tell things to Diana. The excitement of being on the way to visit

Diana, to be actually going to see the farm, was almost too much to bear. She would have to get the address from the post office because a box number and a district number was the only address Diana used on her letters.

Dear Diana, Miss Peabody wrote, resting the little pad of notepaper on her handbag. Dear Diana, you would have laughed, with my dinner just now I nearly ate the *Lavenda-rette*, my *Serviette Rafraichissante*, *Fazzoletto Rinfrescante*, *Verfrissing-soekje*, *Erfrischungstuch*. She paused, holding her pen.

It was exciting to be skimming over the tops of all these places, all on a perfumed paper towel so to speak!

Right across the world on a tissue.

Miss Peabody slept.

"She was in the middle of a sentence when she died," the Matron of the nursing home said. "Your letters gave her a great deal of pleasure," she said, "she spent a lot of time making notes for her replies. As you know, she was a writer, she spent most of her time on the verandah, there's her table and her chair, I haven't moved anything yet. She sat there writing her letters to you. How do you like your tea?"

"Just as it comes thank you," Miss Peabody drank her tea quickly. It was bitter. Tea in Australia did not taste the same. Perhaps she had jet lag or whatever it was called.

"It's the water," Miss Flourish, the Matron, explained, "people can't stand it when they first come here, but after a bit you don't notice its awfulness. It's deep well water and has all sorts of things in it, salts and minerals, nothing harmful of course but just this ghastly taste. Takes about a year to get used to it really." Miss Flourish smiled, "have another piece of my upside down cake."

"Thank you," Miss Peabody wanted to ask about Diana. She did not know what she wanted to ask. It was a shock to have arrived at the place which she thought was Diana's farm to find it was a small private hospital. It was a very pretty place, "Flowermead", a beautiful setting in a rose garden. Lorraine Lee climbing over trellis work and round the verandah posts and up to the gables of the house, into the iron roof and piercing the point of the gable so that pink roses burst in flowering bunches wherever there were imperfect joins in the roofing iron. The garden lawns sloped to the grassy edge of a river, full now, the Matron explained, because of the good early rains.

"She liked to be able to hear the creek running, that's why I gave her this room on this side of the house. The paddock's flooded and the water is the last thing to get dark. See how it holds the last light of the sun and it gleams — she loved that. She sat here hour upon hour listening to the music of the water and to the noise of the frogs. They haven't started yet but they'll make their rattling and croaking later on." Miss Flourish poured more tea for herself. "This place reminded her of her farm, d'you see, before she had the accident."

"Accident?"

"Years ago. She was thrown from a horse, damaged her spine. She was a great rider. She rode hard, had two horses die under her. They had to be shot. Wonder she wasn't hurt, badly hurt, years before. Had things on her mind. An unhappiness. We never knew. Then arthritis set in. Finally it was her heart. She had a heart you know . . ."

Miss Peabody, who was not good at remembering anything, suddenly thought of the typed page in one of the letters, something which did not fit in, about numerous operations. She tried to think. So that was it! Diana never once complained or let her know that she was ill and in pain.

But then Diana was a Goddess. Artemis.

Miss Peabody, after the excitement of looking forward to the meeting with Diana, taking Diana by surprise, making the long journey with all this promise of pleasure stored inside herself, had to understand at once that she would never be able to see Diana, never speak with her. She would not miss that since she had never been able to meet and speak. The sudden and strange bereavement was of not being able to think about and compose and write the letters to Diana. For some time now she had been writing and telling her everything and, because of this, life had become suddenly pleasant. And then too there were the letters from Diana. She had looked forward to them with eagerness. Because of the letters Miss Peabody had known happiness.

"I was looking forward . . . " she began, and then she cried. Miss Flourish, trying to comfort her, heaped cake on her plate. She patted Miss Peabody's quivering shoulder. She bit and chewed an apple noisily to somehow make things ordinary and all right.

"Please don't cry," Miss Flourish said. She knew a great deal about the shocks people had during their lives. It was best to let them cry but, at the same time, it was necessary to murmur phrases like, "please don't cry", as part of the ritual.

Rain was falling and drops trembled along the trellis of rose leaves and large drops gathered on the wet roses and hung, tremulous, before falling. The verandah and the bare table and the empty chair all looked serene and peaceful. Birds would sing after the rain. Miss Flourish reminded Miss Peabody about the birds. The clumps of reeds round the flood water darkened and the water itself shone with a yellow bronzed light. It was like an ornamental lake, Miss Peabody raised her tear swollen face to make a polite remark about the swamp. Miss Flourish assured her it was only a mistake in drainage. The problem was seasonal, the paddock was not always under water like that.

Miss Peabody could not stop crying. It was as if all the loneliness of years welled within her and spilled over in the tears. She tried to explain to Miss Flourish about her holiday and why she had come.

Miss Flourish rang the bell and asked the gardener, who answered it, to light a fire in the room. The firelight was attractive. Miss Flourish thought Miss Peabody should have a few days rest. She could occupy the room for a short time. "Flowermead", she said, could offer the room for a few days.

"Read your letter, it is not quite finished," she said, "if you remember I told you Diana died in the middle of a sentence." She smiled at Miss Peabody.

Diana Hopewell's room was clean and comfortable. It was spacious too and the fire was pleasant company. Miss Flourish folded back the counterpane.

"Read your letter," she said again to Miss Peabody. "I'll have something sent in to you on a tray," she said. She put her head out of the door.

"Patterson!" she called, "bring in some more fire logs. And tell Mavis to do a tray for room ten." She turned back into the room. "Fish or eggs?" she asked, "brown bread or white?"

"Oh it doesn't matter," Miss Peabody said, "really don't go to any trouble for me."

"No trouble at all," Miss Flourish said, "Patterson!" she bawled into the passage, "Fish and eggs for room ten, brown bread and hurry with the firewood!"

Miss Peabody, with her tray beside her on a low table by the fire, began to feel rested. The bed looked comfortable. The place was quiet. She heard the river outside, a gentle sound of water flowing. Tomorrow she would take a walk and have a look at the garden. Perhaps later she would look at Diana's property. Miss Flourish seemed very kind. Miss Peabody liked to think that Diana had been with someone kind. Perhaps the two women were friends.

A great writer, whose name escapes me for the moment, once wrote something about continuing life at a lower level of expectation, the novelist's writing covered the pages, the words running into each other as if she had been writing as quickly as possible. Perhaps something of this will be apparent by the end of the book, she wrote, it interests me very much that people can and do change their level of expectation.

Why ever would Mr Frome want the paddock or part of it, this thought is uppermost in Miss Thorne's mind as she carves the cold meat. She is suffering from jet lag, sorry, I'll underline that; the novelist did so with violet ink.

It is her, Miss Thorne's, custom to enter the kitchen before eight in the morning with an apron tied across her wide blue skirt to trim and carve the cold sideboards for Sunday luncheon. What is not consumed during that meal reappears on Monday evening and, if still left over, on the following Wednesday for lunch.

For a moment Ernest Frome and the paddock take second place in Miss Thorne's mind. She has just been demonstrating a weight reducing exercise to the overweight girls who have embarked with her on the Pine Heights lemon and oatmeal diet. Seriously intent on improving their thick waists Miss Thorne demonstrated the special exercise. Something so terrible happened during the demonstration that Miss Thorne makes up her mind that she must never perform this strenuous exercise in public again.

The Aubergine twins are practising Mozart on the pantry piano.

I can't have a married woman let loose in the Boarding House, Miss Thorne says to herself for the hundredth time. She is not sure, of course, whether Gwenda is returning to school as Gwendaline Manners or Gwendaline Frome. That Gwenda and Debbie will be three weeks late suggests that Mr Frome plans to carry out his intention with a special licence and the blessings of Debbie's grandmother and heaven knows how many other perfectly frightful Frome relatives.

And then there's the honeymoon. He, that man, is sure to want that. Miss Thorne shudders at the thought. She is quite honest with herself as her sharp knife slides through the innocent but tough meat.

"I suppose I really cannot tolerate the idea of Gwen—— of the gel being actually married to that man." She arranges the sliced meat in neat rows on the platter. In spite of everything the meat has an appetizing smell. It is satisfactory, this neat placing of the pieces of meat.

"I suppose I should have ... but what could I ... " Miss Thorne goes on talking to herself,

She has thrown herself away upon that boor from sheer ignorance that better individuals existed ... I must beware how I cause her to regret her choice.

The Aubergine Mozart is reasonable. Not too many false notes. Miss Thorne smiles with satisfaction. With judicious serving, there will be enough meat for three meals. And then, those lines from Emily Brontë coming into her head like that. A perfect gift.

She has thrown herself away upon the boor from sheer ignorance that better individuals existed. Year Eleven could write something from the lines for their creative writing exercise. Who knows some gel might even perceive something and receive, in this way, timely warning.

It takes a few hours to recover from the long flight from London. Miss Thorne is aware of an inability to dwell with any kind of real concentration on a subject. She finds herself thinking of the young man in the seat next to hers. In reply to a pleasant remark from Miss Thorne that hours spent in air travel which might be tedious were in fact not if the traveller equipped himself with enlightening reading material, he lent her the journal he had himself been reading. The magazine dealt with literary criticism and there were some reviews of present day writers.

"Just my sort of reading," she had smiled at the young man.

Miss Thorne read,

. . . The discussion falls on the concept of structuralist reading and the exposure of the artistic process as being an achievement, on semantic levels, of harmonious surfaces built on insoluble conflicts, for example, the lexical, the grammatical and syntactic levels, with an ideological solution to the contradictions in the mode of discourse, the angle of narration and the symbolic structure of a culture . . .

Looking back now from the edge of the kitchen table she remembers her extraordinary feelings, extraordinary because she is unaccustomed to being unable to understand anything she reads. It is the same with foreign languages. Being able to understand and speak fluently (if slowly at times) several, she has had to realize, with surprise, that there are tongues so foreign that she does not know to which country they belong.

The article and her lack of comprehension which she recalls makes her, for a moment, doubt her own position, particularly as she is, because of not understanding what was being discussed, unable to remember any words or phrases. She does remember vaguely reading another statement that being a character in a novel is apparently not being a character at all.

Such ways of thinking are too much for her. Dizzily she returns to the meat. The meat is there and she is cutting it.

The thoughts of the day are not so heavy after all. Miss Thorne will be lunching in her own apartment, upstairs in the Boarding House, with Miss Snowdon. She is looking forward to spending some time with her friend. She is thankful to be safely back at school. It has an air of safety as a fortress, well maintained, might have. Even if Bales does shake his head whenever he meets her, as she, defying gravity, sails uphill, gigantic in black oiled silk, between the straining, dripping pines, going up the fragrant, pine-needly, rainsoaked path from the Boarding House to the School House. He shakes his head.

"An early tempest of a winter and us only two weeks into

the term," he says as they pass each other. "Epidedemic!" he says, "Epidedemics!" Miss Thorne understands that it is his way of greeting her as another person might say, "Good morning".

Miss Thorne knows that all eight children of the three junior mistresses are down with measles. Bales is quite right to shake his head and his word of greeting is correctly chosen.

Still thinking about Mr Frome and wondering about his wish for her paddock, or part of it, Miss Thorne puts away her knife and the meat. She gives Mrs Bales her instructions for the day.

Mrs Bales who is, by self declaration, deaf and tone deaf does not hear either these or the crashing discords of the next pupil who is practising in the pantry before breakfast.

At this hour of the morning the school resounds with piano practice of varying degrees of inability. Pianos are all over the place in strategic positions. Purrings of Chopin come from the Visitors' Room, a Scott Joplin revival pounds from the top landing, the Aubergine twins, feeling unable to give up their Mozart, unwillingly leave the pantry piano to the scales and arpeggios of the next student and continue their music on the battered piano in the old ground floor bathroom where those who have overslept are still taking late showers and Bales, wanting to be finished with the cleaning, is hosing and mopping the floors. Fortunately, he too is tone deaf, and deaf too to the strangely chosen words of complaint from the well-bred daughters of the rich.

Miss Thorne is running a little late for her luncheon engagement with Miss Snowdon. She wants to address the girls and does so in the dining hall while they are sitting with their plates of cold meat and beetroot before them. She walks between the tables bearing the large plate of cold mutton. She tells them, as she walks, the life history of the lamb. She tells them there is nothing wrong with the meat.

Remembering the dripping envelope returned to the school from the post office last term,

"There is absooty nothing wrong with this meat," she says in a contralto, resonant, and known to be dangerous. "I will not have any gel sending slices of this excellent meat and gravy through the post to their parents." She explains that if they wish to make any complaints there is a special time set aside every week for complaints. She reminds the four new girls that they are invited to her study for afternoon tea at four o'clock.

"I am sure we shall get to know one another very well," she says, her voice changing to a soft growl. "Please go on now with your meal."

Surrounded by the remains of a crayfish and a pleasant lettuce salad, Miss Thorne lights one of her neglected little black cigars.

"Brandy deah?"

"No thank you Prickles. I have to address the first year student nurses at four."

"There's plenty of time deah."

"Well, perhaps just a teeny one then."

"Down the hatch!"

The study is warm with a lively fire. Satisfactory rain is pouring down the outside of the window.

"But when, I ask you, but when the marriage bed becomes a sick bed, what then?"

"Very dramatic Prickles. I suppose it is your literary leanings, your literary bent."

"Snow! Cliché of the worst sort!"

"Yes Prickles. Sorry! But seriously the marriage bed can be a sick bed or even an empty bed at any age, no matter about age difference. And often is during a lifetime."

"True Snow! There are things, though, worse than illness or death."

"Very unprofitable thoughts Prickles, especially at this stage of the gel's life."

"Yes I know Snow. But old age Snow, the approach to old age. Crabbed old age."

"A quotation?"

"No, perhaps a little, but misquoted out of context."

"How's Edge?" Miss Snowdon settles her bulk more comfortably while Miss Thorne cleans her nose.

"Well as you know, Snow, we lorst each other in London. Such a simple place really for meetings. One of those silly misunderstandings. I'd been to get you the little piece of Dresden . . . "

Miss Snowdon makes suitable noises of appreciation in the past tense over the already given gift.

"One of those silly misunderstandings! I spoke to her last night. 'Phone, it'll cost the earth," Miss Thorne gives a little shrug to do with mounting expenses about which it is not possible to do anything.

"I got through finally. God, the Italian exchanges!"

"Where is she now?"

"Rome. She's had to break her journey. She put her back out or something equally mysterious. You know Edge, she can't put her feet out of bed without stepping into some kind of disaster! She was taken orf the 'plane in Rome in agony. She's in hospital, a place on the outskirts high up. She says she's overlooking the Viale Glorioso and has a view of the Vatican. All very auspicious. But you know Edge, she might have it all wrong. She's probably gazing piously at the meat works or some other useful but hideous place."

"I suppose if she thinks it's the Vatican, that's enough."

"Yes, you're right Snow. And the other thing that comes to my mind is that surely all hospitals in Rome will have at least one window either looking towards St Peter's or the Vatican — even if the view is obliterated by buildings and monuments . . . "

"What's wrong with Edgely?"

"Oh nothing that a few weeks on traction and bed-pans won't put right."

"And Gwenda?"

"I've told you Everything Snow."

"Sorry Prickles."

"Oh, it's all right Snow. Let's have another brandy deah!"

"Down the hatch!" Both women stare pensively into the fire glow. Relaxed, they have hitched up their rather formal skirts and sit with their large knees apart.

"Then there's Frome," Miss Thorne says, "wanting to buy my paddock. I suppose I'll consider his offer . . . but why would he want it?"

"Perhaps he wants to build a house there, I mean it would be close for the gel, for Gwenda to slip across to school for her arithmetic and so on."

"Snow! How can you!"

"Sorry, Sorry Prickles deah, but you do have to admit . . ."

"God knows what he wants, Snow. But anything that man wants he seems to get." Miss Thorne pauses. "He'll probably turn up on the night of the bra burning ceremony presuming that I am jumping at his offer."

"Well, aren't you?" Miss Snowdon gives a little smile and looks sideways at her friend.

Miss Thorne, reflecting on Mr Frome, has an absurd picture, a series of pictures flashing through her mind. The huge fire in the paddock and the gels chanting and dancing, rings of fire running on the grass, and Mr Frome, leaving the magic circle, round the fire, to steal upstairs to say "good night" to Gwenda before leaving her. A suburban Wotan poignantly saying farewell to a clumsy but pleasant schoolgirl.

"Of course," Miss Thorne says to Miss Snowdon, "I simply can't have a man going upstairs in the Boarding House to the dorm. I mean men never go there except the doctor, occasionally, for an earache or something like that. And, I suppose, in the event of a sudden death, a priest might be permitted. But we have never had anyone die at Pine Heights . . ."

"That is certainly to your credit Prickles."

"Snow! You are in an extraordinarily flippant mood."

"Sorry Prickles!" Miss Snowdon is laughing. "It's the idea of the gel and Mr Frome, I mean your idea . . . " Miss Snowdon is silent. Both women stare into the fire. Miss Thorne continues to reflect on Mr Frome, that is, after she has, in her mind, turned him out of the dormitory. She is thinking of all the ways in which all kinds of people can benefit from his common sense and his money, if they are prepared to do things his way.

"By the way," Miss Thorne tosses off her brandy and breathes out a cloud of smoke, "I've promised Edge Grinzing next year."

"Oh Jolly Good! Count me in." Miss Snowdon says, "it'll be something to look forward to."

"I can't help, all the same, going over it in my mind," Miss Thorne murmurs, "I mean, why ever would Mr Frome, that man, want the paddock. There's always the realization that

Miss Peabody, coming to the end of the letter which was in the middle of the unfinished sentence, looked out of the window at the tall trees. They were, she was sure, taller than the English elms. The dark heads of foliage were quite still. The flood water gleamed, shining with colourless light. The edges of the paddock and the reeds along the river were black. Only the drainage mistake, the water poured over the grass like a libation, was light. Beyond, between banks of night coloured cloud, and between the silent tree tops, there was a space in that part of the sky which was either holding light still from the other side of the horizon or gathering a silvery lightness from the quickly rising moon. Below that harbour in the sky was where Diana's place must be.

Miss Peabody, for a moment, thought of Kingston Avenue. She dismissed the thought instantly. Mrs Brewer had promised to keep an eye on the empty house. The promise was more for her dead friend, Mrs Peabody, she made it quite clear to Dorothy that it was for her mother's sake she would watch over the house. Putting Kingston Avenue out of her mind completely, Miss Peabody thought that Miss Flourish would possibly go with her to see Diana's farm.

There were enormous possibilities. She had only to look at her bulging handbag. There was no one at all to tell things to. No one knew all that was contained in her handbag.

Miss Peabody, sitting at the window with the fire pleasantly warm and lively behind her and the clean bed, turned down, ready for her when she wanted it, began to go over things in her mind. She was thinking: Miss Thorne's coloured dressed gown cord, the novelist had not reached the place in the writing where it would be mentioned again. Miss Flourish looked the sort of person who would possess such a cord, something suitable for Othello. There was the subject of jealousy too. People, until they experienced jealousy, had no knowledge of what it felt like to be jealous. Perhaps the theme was to have been developed between Gwenda and Debbie?

Why ever would Mr Frome want the paddock. There's always the realization that . . .

The sky harbour slipped from Miss Peabody's mind. It was a comfortable memory of something she liked, the idea of going to see Diana's farm, but she knew it would never be necessary to actually make the effort to go there.

Miss Flourish would be sure to know where it was possible to get a typewriter. Miss Peabody, though she made abysmal typing errors, knew she could type well enough. All she really needed to enter into her inheritance was a title.

MORE ABOUT PENGUINS, PELICANS,
PEREGRINES AND PUFFINS

For further information about books available from Penguins please write to Dept EP, Penguin Books Ltd, Harmondsworth, Middlesex UB7 0DA.

In the U.S.A.: For a complete list of books available from Penguins in the United States write to Dept DG, Penguin Books, 299 Murray Hill Parkway, East Rutherford, New Jersey 07073.

In Canada: For a complete list of books available from Penguins in Canada write to Penguin Books Canada Ltd, 2801 John Street, Markham, Ontario L3R 1B4.

In Australia: For a complete list of books available from Penguins in Australia write to the Marketing Department, Penguin Books Australia Ltd, P.O. Box 257, Ringwood, Victoria 3134.

In New Zealand: For a complete list of books available from Penguins in New Zealand write to the Marketing Department, Penguin Books (N.Z.) Ltd, Private Bag, Takapuna, Auckland 9.

In India: For a complete list of books available from Penguins in India write to Penguin Overseas Ltd, 706 Eros Apartments, 56 Nehru Place, New Delhi 110019.

KING PENGUIN

☐ *Selected Poems* **Tony Harrison** £3.95

Poetry Book Society Recommendation. 'One of the few modern poets who actually has the gift of composing poetry' – James Fenton in the *Sunday Times*

☐ *The Book of Laughter and Forgetting*
Milan Kundera £3.95

'A whirling dance of a book . . . a masterpiece full of angels, terror, ostriches and love . . . No question about it. The most important novel published in Britain this year' – Salman Rushdie in the *Sunday Times*

☐ *The Sea of Fertility* **Yukio Mishima** £9.95

Containing *Spring Snow, Runaway Horses, The Temple of Dawn* and *The Decay of the Angel*: 'These four remarkable novels are the most complete vision we have of Japan in the twentieth century' – Paul Theroux

☐ *The Hawthorne Goddess* **Glyn Hughes** £2.95

Set in eighteenth century Yorkshire where 'the heroine, Anne Wylde, represents the doom of nature and the land . . . Hughes has an arresting style, both rich and abrupt' – *The Times*

☐ *A Confederacy of Dunces* **John Kennedy Toole** £3.95

In this Pulitzer Prize-winning novel, in the bulky figure of Ignatius J. Reilly an immortal comic character is born. 'I succumbed, stunned and seduced . . . it is a masterwork of comedy' – *The New York Times*

☐ *The Last of the Just* **André Schwartz-Bart** £3.95

The story of Ernie Levy, the last of the just, who was killed at Auschwitz in 1943: 'An outstanding achievement, of an altogether different order from even the best of earlier novels which have attempted this theme' – John Gross in the *Sunday Telegraph*

KING PENGUIN

☐ *The White Hotel* **D. M. Thomas**   £3.95

'A major artist has once more appeared', declared the *Spectator* on the publication of this acclaimed, now famous novel which recreates the imagined case history of one of Freud's woman patients.

☐ *Dangerous Play: Poems 1974–1984*
   Andrew Motion   £2.95

Winner of the John Llewelyn Rhys Memorial Prize. Poems and an autobiographical prose piece, *Skating*, by the poet acclaimed in the *TLS* as 'a natural heir to the tradition of Edward Thomas and Ivor Gurney'.

☐ *A Time to Dance* **Bernard MacLaverty**   £2.50

Ten stories, including 'My Dear Palestrina' and 'Phonefun Limited', by the author of *Cal*: 'A writer who has a real affinity with the short story form' – *The Times Literary Supplement*

☐ *Keepers of the House* **Lisa St Aubin de Terán**   £2.95

Seventeen-year-old Lydia Sinclair marries Don Diego Beltrán and goes to live on his family's vast, decaying Andean farm. This exotic and flamboyant first novel won the Somerset Maugham Award.

☐ *The Deptford Trilogy* **Robertson Davies**   £5.95

'Who killed Boy Staunton?' – around this central mystery is woven an exhilarating and cunningly contrived trilogy of novels: *Fifth Business, The Manticore* and *World of Wonders*.

☐ *The Stories of William Trevor*   £5.95

'Trevor packs into each separate five or six thousand words more richness, more laughter, more ache, more multifarious human-ness than many good writers manage to get into a whole novel' – *Punch*. 'Classics of the genre' – Auberon Waugh

A CHOICE OF PENGUINS

☐ *Small World* **David Lodge** £2.50

A jet-propelled academic romance, sequel to *Changing Places*. 'A new comic débâcle on every page' – *The Times*. 'Here is everything one expects from Lodge but three times as entertaining as anything he has written before' – *Sunday Telegraph*

☐ *The Neverending Story* **Michael Ende** £3.95

The international bestseller, now a major film: 'A tale of magical adventure, pursuit and delay, danger, suspense, triumph' – *The Times Literary Supplement*

☐ *The Sword of Honour Trilogy* **Evelyn Waugh** £3.95

Containing *Men at Arms, Officers and Gentlemen* and *Unconditional Surrender*, the trilogy described by Cyril Connolly as 'unquestionably the finest novels to have come out of the war'.

☐ *The Honorary Consul* **Graham Greene** £2.50

In a provincial Argentinian town, a group of revolutionaries kidnap the wrong man . . . 'The tension never relaxes and one reads hungrily from page to page, dreading the moment it will all end' – Auberon Waugh in the *Evening Standard*

☐ *The First Rumpole Omnibus* **John Mortimer** £4.95

Containing *Rumpole of the Bailey, The Trials of Rumpole* and *Rumpole's Return*. 'A fruity, foxy masterpiece, defender of our wilting faith in mankind' – *Sunday Times*

☐ *Scandal* **A. N. Wilson** £2.25

Sexual peccadillos, treason and blackmail are all ingredients on the boil in A. N. Wilson's new, *cordon noir* comedy. 'Drily witty, deliciously nasty' – *Sunday Telegraph*

A CHOICE OF PENGUINS

☐ *Stanley and the Women* **Kingsley Amis** £2.50

'Very good, very powerful ... beautifully written ... This is Amis *père* at his best' – Anthony Burgess in the *Observer*. 'Everybody should read it' – *Daily Mail*

☐ *The Mysterious Mr Ripley* **Patricia Highsmith** £4.95

Containing *The Talented Mr Ripley, Ripley Underground* and *Ripley's Game*. 'Patricia Highsmith is the poet of apprehension' – Graham Greene. 'The Ripley books are marvellously, insanely readable' – *The Times*

☐ *Earthly Powers* **Anthony Burgess** £4.95

'Crowded, crammed, bursting with manic erudition, garlicky puns, omnilingual jokes ... (a novel) which meshes the real and personalized history of the twentieth century' – Martin Amis

☐ *Life & Times of Michael K* **J. M. Coetzee** £2.95

The Booker Prize-winning novel: 'It is hard to convey ... just what Coetzee's special quality is. His writing gives off whiffs of Conrad, of Nabokov, of Golding, of the Paul Theroux of *The Mosquito Coast*. But he is none of these, he is a harsh, compelling new voice' – Victoria Glendinning

☐ *The Stories of William Trevor* £5.95

'Trevor packs into each separate five or six thousand words more richness, more laughter, more ache, more multifarious human-ness than many good writers manage to get into a whole novel' – *Punch*

☐ *The Book of Laughter and Forgetting*
Milan Kundera £3.95

'A whirling dance of a book ... a masterpiece full of angels, terror, ostriches and love ... No question about it. The most important novel published in Britain this year' – Salman Rushdie

A CHOICE OF PENGUINS

☐ **_Further Chronicles of Fairacre_ 'Miss Read'** £3.95

Full of humour, warmth and charm, these four novels – _Miss Clare Remembers, Over the Gate, The Fairacre Festival_ and _Emily Davis_ – make up an unforgettable picture of English village life.

☐ **_Callanish_ William Horwood** £1.95

From the acclaimed author of _Duncton Wood_, this is the haunting story of Creggan, the captured golden eagle, and his struggle to be free.

☐ **_Act of Darkness_ Francis King** £2.50

Anglo-India in the 1930s, where a peculiarly vicious murder triggers 'A terrific mystery story . . . a darkly luminous parable about innocence and evil' – _The New York Times_. 'Brilliantly successful' – _Daily Mail_. 'Unputdownable' – _Standard_

☐ **_Death in Cyprus_ M. M. Kaye** £1.95

Holidaying on Aphrodite's beautiful island, Amanda finds herself caught up in a murder mystery in which no one, not even the attractive painter Steven Howard, is quite what they seem . . .

☐ **_Lace_ Shirley Conran** £2.95

Lace is, quite simply, a publishing sensation: the story of Judy, Kate, Pagan and Maxine; the bestselling novel that teaches men about women, and women about themselves. 'Riches, bitches, sex and jetsetters' locations – they're all there' – _Sunday Express_

A CHOICE OF PENGUINS

☐ **West of Sunset** Dirk Bogarde £1.95

'His virtues as a writer are precisely those which make him the most compelling screen actor of his generation,' is what *The Times* said about Bogarde's savage, funny, romantic novel set in the gaudy wastes of Los Angeles.

☐ **The Riverside Villas Murder** Kingsley Amis £1.95

Marital duplicity, sexual discovery and murder with a thirties back-cloth: 'Amis in top form' – *The Times*. 'Delectable from page to page . . . effortlessly witty' – C. P. Snow in the *Financial Times*

☐ **A Dark and Distant Shore** Reay Tannahill £3.95

Vilia is the unforgettable heroine, Kinveil Castle is her destiny, in this full-blooded saga spanning a century of Victoriana, empire, hatreds and love affairs. 'A marvellous blend of *Gone with the Wind* and *The Thorn Birds*. You will enjoy every page' – *Daily Mirror*

☐ **Kingsley's Touch** John Collee £1.95

'Gripping . . . I recommend this chilling and elegantly written medical thriller' – *Daily Express*. 'An absolutely outstanding storyteller' – *Daily Telegraph*

☐ **The Far Pavilions** M. M. Kaye £4.95

Holding all the romance and high adventure of nineteenth-century India, M. M. Kaye's magnificent, now famous, novel has at its heart the passionate love of an Englishman for Juli, his Indian princess. 'Wildly exciting' – *Daily Telegraph*

PENGUIN OMNIBUSES

☐ **_Victorian Villainies_**   £5.95

Fraud, murder, political intrigue and horror are the ingredients of these four Victorian thrillers, selected by Hugh Greene and Graham Greene.

☐ **_The Balkan Trilogy_ Olivia Manning**   £5.95

This acclaimed trilogy – _The Great Fortune, The Spoilt City_ and _Friends and Heroes_ – is the portrait of a marriage, and an exciting recreation of civilian life in the Second World War. 'It amuses, it diverts, and it informs' – Frederick Raphael

☐ **_The Penguin Collected Stories of Isaac Bashevis Singer_**   £5.95

Forty-seven marvellous tales of Jewish magic, faith and exile. 'Never was the Nobel Prize more deserved . . . He belongs with the giants' – _Sunday Times_

☐ **_The Penguin Essays of George Orwell_**   £4.95

Famous pieces on 'The Decline of the English Murder', 'Shooting an Elephant', political issues and P. G. Wodehouse feature in this edition of forty-one essays, criticism and sketches – all classics of English prose.

☐ **_Further Chronicles of Fairacre_ 'Miss Read'**   £3.95

Full of humour, warmth and charm, these four novels – _Miss Clare Remembers, Over the Gate, The Fairacre Festival_ and _Emily Davis_ – make up an unforgettable picture of English village life.

☐ **_The Penguin Complete Sherlock Holmes_ Sir Arthur Conan Doyle**   £5.95

With the fifty-six classic short stories, plus _A Study in Scarlet, The Sign of Four, The Hound of the Baskervilles_ and _The Valley of Fear_, this volume contains the remarkable career of Baker Street's most famous resident.

PENGUIN OMNIBUSES

☐ **Life with Jeeves P. G. Wodehouse**   £3.95

Containing *Right Ho, Jeeves, The Inimitable Jeeves* and *Very Good, Jeeves!* in which Wodehouse lures us, once again, into the evergreen world of Bertie Wooster, his terrifying Aunt Agatha, his man Jeeves and other eggs, good and bad.

☐ **The Penguin Book of Ghost Stories**   £4.95

An anthology to set the spine tingling, including stories by Zola, Kleist, Sir Walter Scott, M. R. James, Elizabeth Bowen and A. S. Byatt.

☐ **The Penguin Book of Horror Stories**   £4.95

Including stories by Maupassant, Poe, Gautier, Conan Doyle, L. P. Hartley and Ray Bradbury, in a selection of the most horrifying horror from the eighteenth century to the present day.

☐ **The Penguin Complete Novels of Jane Austen**   £5.95

Containing the seven great novels: *Sense and Sensibility, Pride and Prejudice, Mansfield Park, Emma, Northanger Abbey, Persuasion* and *Lady Susan*.

☐ **Perfick, Perfick! H. E. Bates**   £4.95

The adventures of the irrepressible Larkin family, in four novels: *The Darling Buds of May, A Breath of French Air, When the Green Woods Laugh* and *Oh! To Be in England*.

☐ **Famous Trials**
Harry Hodge and James H. Hodge   £3.95

From Madeleine Smith to Dr Crippen and Lord Haw-Haw, this volume contains the most sensational murder and treason trials, selected by John Mortimer from the classic Penguin Famous Trials series.

ENGLISH AND AMERICAN
LITERATURE IN PENGUINS

☐ *Main Street* **Sinclair Lewis**   £4.95

The novel that added an immortal chapter to the literature of America's Mid-West, *Main Street* contains the comic essence of Main Streets everywhere.

☐ *The Compleat Angler* **Izaak Walton**   £2.50

A celebration of the countryside, and the superiority of those in 1653, as now, who love *quietnesse, vertue* and, above all, *Angling*. 'No fish, however coarse, could wish for a doughtier champion than Izaak Walton' – Lord Home

☐ *The Portrait of a Lady* **Henry James**   £2.50

'One of the two most brilliant novels in the language', according to F. R. Leavis, James's masterpiece tells the story of a young American heiress, prey to fortune-hunters but not without a will of her own.

☐ *Hangover Square* **Patrick Hamilton**   £3.95

Part love story, part thriller, and set in the publands of London's Earls Court, this novel caught the conversational tone of a whole generation in the uneasy months before the Second World War.

☐ *The Rainbow* **D. H. Lawrence**   £2.50

Written between *Sons and Lovers* and *Women in Love*, *The Rainbow* covers three generations of Brangwens, a yeoman family living on the borders of Nottinghamshire.

☐ *Vindication of the Rights of Woman*
Mary Wollstonecraft   £2.95

Although Walpole once called her 'a hyena in petticoats', Mary Wollstonecraft's vision was such that modern feminists continue to go back and debate the arguments so powerfully set down here.